Dedicated to all domestic violence survivors

DOMESTIC VIOLENCE SUPPORT

If you or anyone you know is in danger and needs help please contact The Domestic Violence Hotline advocates are available 24/7 at 1-800-799-SAFE (7233)

ACKNOWLEDGEMENTS

First and foremost I want to thank God for all his blessings he has given to me and my family.

This feeling as I write this is surreal. BOOK 10 wow. I have followed my dreams and really published not just one book but 10. Thank you to all my family and friends for the support it is greatly appreciated.

I personally thank all the readers from the bottom of my heart for all the support. I wouldn't be at book ten without you all.

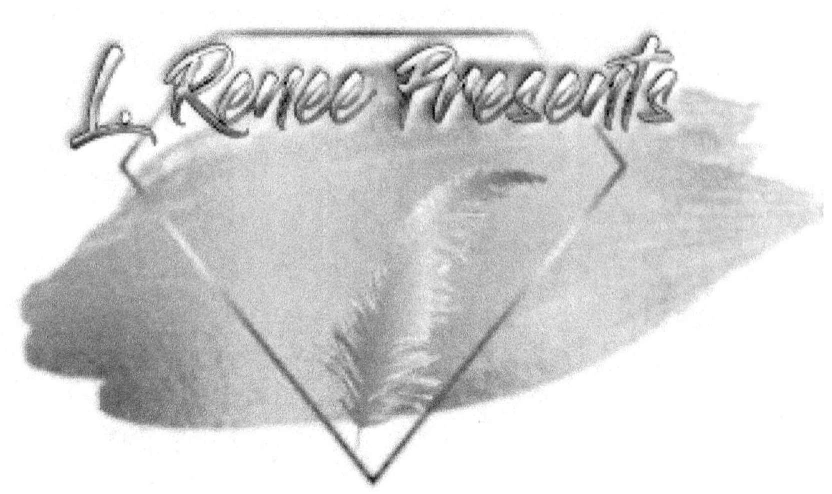
L. Renee Presents

CODE BLUE:
Tales of A Shattered Heart

The sound of the city was like no other sound you could get anywhere else. The chaos was calming, surprisingly, which was why I was currently losing my damn mind out here in the south. My mother, Gladys, loved it, though. So, for her, I was here in Savannah, GA to visit for a few days. She moved here a year ago to take care of my grandparents. My mother was the oldest of 3 kids and basically helped to raise her siblings. I was an only child, as far as I knew, since I never met my daddy. My mother wouldn't speak much on my dad but stated I would know about him when it was safe for her to tell me. I, to this day, didn't understand what that meant, but I left well enough alone and just lived. My mother did ok for us, and I appreciated and loved her dearly. My mother only had one boyfriend, bitch ass, Clyde, my whole life, and he was only around from when I was 4 until I was 10.

My mother was his doormat and punching bag, and when I threatened to kill myself, she knew then she had to get us away from him. He actually was spending some years behind bars right now for the last time he decided to beat on my momma. He ended up putting her in the hospital, and I helped put his ass in jail. I had come home one night from my best friend, Skai's, house when I found my mother getting beat with a belt, as she dripped soaking wet and was naked. I pulled out the cell phone my mother had given to me and recorded everything until he began to deliver punches to her beautiful face. I couldn't take anymore, so I used the Taser and bat my momma left under my bed for me, and I tasered him on the highest setting. Once he was on the floor, I delivered multiple hits with the bat I had.

I then called the police. When the police arrived, I gave them everything they needed, and he had been locked away for the last 8 years. He had warrants and shit for other things too, so combined, he faced time that would keep us safe.

For so long, it had been just me and my momma, but I would love for her to find a nice man and live happy. My mother had me at 18 after being with my father for 5 years, and no one after until Clyde—and no one after Clyde that I know of. My mother raised me alone and on her own with help from my grandparents, Percy and Gloria, Uncle Percy Jr., and my favorite person, who always baby sat me, Auntie Giselle. Giselle didn't have any kids, and she spoiled me like I was hers.

Once I turned 16, she started teaching me all about not letting these guys play me. *Play or be played* was her motto, and she always told me no niece of hers was gon' be played. I loved hanging with her and her friends because they were older, and they were always out partying and living life. Giselle had niggas for days, but she had her own hustle going. She was a tattoo artist in New York, and she made things happen for herself. I had to get up there to visit her soon. If she had it her way, I'd be living there in the Big Apple with her. I knew there wasn't much here for me in Buffalo, but eventually, I had plans on getting out of here once I stacked up enough money. I knew for sure that this country ass town wasn't the move for me, though. It was cool to visit and come spend time with my mom and grandparents, but I still needed some excitement—some noise, dirty air, and sirens in the distance.

I was losing my mind with these crickets and bird chirping, old ladies humming, and the awful smell of grass and fertilizer. I chose to skip the trip to town to go shopping and decided to catch up on some of my ratchet TV shows. I attempted to watch TV as planned, but the only channels my grandparents had were 2, 4, and 7.

"You have got to be fucking kidding me," I whined out loud to no one but my damn self.

I was beyond ready to get out of here. I had two more days of this prison vacation, then I was back to my stomping grounds. I was a City Girl at heart. Point, blank, period, and it was no way around it. This country shit was for the birds. *Literally.*

I sat locked in my daughter's closet hiding from my drunk ass baby father, Rico. This was an everyday thing and had been for the last 2 years of my life. I had no family, and he was all I had out here in this world. But the dark side of him was beginning to be too much to bear. I had my baby girl, Ricaria, a year ago, and I fought through this horrible situation to provide her a roof over her head and essentials like food and clothes. My friend Brie` had Ricaria for me because I had an interview to be a dance instructor for kids at the community center in Brooklyn. I came home to get clothes hoping to be gone before Rico returned because he had lost his money gambling. I was sure to catch his wrath again tonight, and I couldn't take it anymore.

Brie` and my best friend, Gianni, had been telling me to leave him forever, but that was easier said than done. I loved him in the beginning, but now I despised him. I stayed because I was a broke girl from the foster care system with no real family. My foster mother threw me out when I showed up pregnant at 16 by Rico, who was 25 at that time. I lost that baby thanks to Rico delivering his size 10 boot to my stomach repeatedly after I refused to get an abortion. When I was 18, after moving up to Brooklyn from Buffalo, he was ready for me to be his child's mother and here we were now with Ricaria.

I jumped from my thoughts when I heard Rico stumbling

through the house talking shit. I planned to run for it once I knew he was sleep.

I waited damn near an hour and almost dozed off to sleep my damn self when I finally came out of the closet. I tried to stand up, and immediately, a cramp took over my leg sending me crashing to the floor. I wanted to yell out in pain, but I knew not to wake up the drunken beast. He'd be pissed I hid from him and even more pissed I'd woke him up. That would be an ass beating I wasn't built for. I tip toed into the hallway, and I could hear Rico snoring like a bear. I grabbed the overnight bag I stashed in the hallway linen closet and made my way to the front door. I eased the first chain off and then peeked over my shoulder to see if he had heard it. He was sprawled out in his recliner in a wife beater, go figure, a pair of grey sweatpants, and some Cali style house slippers for men. One hung loosely off his foot that was propped over the arm of the recliner, and the other fit snug as it rested on the footrest of the recliner.

I went to slide the second lock, which was the slide latch lock. That one would take some time, as it was old and rusted and sometimes squeaked. I held my breath as I slowly slid the lock over and exhaled once it was at the base. I peeked over my shoulder again, and he still was sleep—with his old raggedy ass. I shook my head at how crazy this was how I had to sneak out of my home. I slowly turned the twist lock on the doorknob and slowly pulled it open. I had one foot out the door before I was snatched by my hood on my hoodie I wore. I almost pissed my pants when I was spun around face to face with Rico. I trembled in fear as he glared down at me, neck veins bulging and pulsating as he breathed heavily. I was scared for my life and most certain he could tell because he burst into a fit of laughter like a lunatic. I was still in between the doorway, and he had not let me go.

"Where the fuck you think you going, Skai?! And where the fuck is my daughter?!" he shouted as spit flew from his mouth.

He had my hood balled into his fist, damn near becoming one with his fingers. I didn't speak. I couldn't speak, but the tears started, and that only caused more laughter from this maniac.

I squeezed my eyes shut to try and stop the tears. Yet before I could open them back, his big ass hand came straight across my left cheek, causing my ear to ring instantly. My hand shot to my stinging face and ear and then another slap to the back of my head came. I tried to crawl away towards the kitchen to get anything to fight back with, but he had knocked me off balance, and I was struggling to get there.

He tried to pull me by my hair, but that was hard considering I now sported a pixie cut, thanks to him. Rico hated my curly hair and how long and flowy it was. He wanted me to wear it bone straight at all times. One day, I had taken Ricaria to the pool, and my hair got wet. It curled right up. The minute I got compliments on it; he went off on me the whole ride home. Once we entered the house, he threatened to cut it all off if I didn't straighten it. It took me hours to straighten my tresses, but I did it.

The next day, he came home with a box relaxer and made me put it in my hair. I cried the whole time. When it was time to rinse it out, he decided to shut the shower water off as a way to teach me a lesson. It wasn't until I screamed and begged for him to let me rinse it out, 'cuz it burned so bad, that he finally let me. But by then, it was too late. All my hair rinsed right out in that shower, and I'd been rocking a pixie finger wave cut, that I had to YouTube how to do, ever since. He must've become frustrated that he didn't have hair to swing me around with like a rag doll anymore because he commenced to kicking and punching me everywhere. I swung and flailed my arms like a windmill and connected with his nose that I was sure I broke.

He doubled over in pain, yet my adrenaline was pumping. So, I hopped up off the floor bouncing around, ready to go toe to toe with his ass, but he was acting like a bitch rocking on his knees. I ran up behind him and delivered a hard kick to his little ass dick before I grabbed the keys, my bag and bolted out that house. I could hear him in the distance screaming in pain.

Even though I was hurting physically from the beating, and internally from all the hurt I had endured, I smiled with satisfaction that I had got his ass this time. I felt strength from that little bit, and that was because I knew I had to get out. I wasn't going back this time, though. I had to make something shake real quick around here so I could live and provide a safe environment for my daughter.

I had just finished feeding Ricaria, and I was starting to worry about Skai. She hadn't answered my calls or texts, and I didn't have enough gas to drive to her apartment and check on her. I decided to give it another hour and then I'd see if my brother, Bilal, could give me a ride over there. I had a few hair appointments late this evening—mostly braids. So, I started getting my work area ready while Ricaria watched *Doc McStuffins* and played with her fake puppy. I couldn't wait for the day Skai would leave this nigga alone and come live with me. I knew I had a small, 2 bedrooms, but we were like sisters. We a make that shit work.

I hated Rico with a passion and hoped one day somebody would knock his ass off. Forgive me, Lord, you know my heart, but he was the damn devil. I was just about to fold a load of clothes when banging at my door startled me. Someone was banging on my door like the police. I rushed to the door and checked the peep hole to see a distraught and disheveled, Skai. I unlocked the door and quickly swung it open, and she rushed in past me plopping down on my futon sofa. She was breathing heavy and damn near hyperventilating.

"Skai, what the hell is going on? What happened?" I asked, nervous that she was harmed in some way.

"Brie, I can't take anymore from his ass. I fought Rico back, and I fled up out of there to here. I just need to stay here while I get on my feet and figure out how I'm going to take care of Ricaria and myself." She cried as she hid her face in the pillow on my futon.

I knew this day would come, and I'd tried for the last year or longer to get her to leave that devil of a man alone. I sat down next to my girl and rubbed her back.

"Skai, you and my God-baby can stay here forever. You know that. We gon' figure this shit out, but I got a job for you tonight. My clients will be here in 30 minutes. You can do the box braids for me and keep the money. I will knock out the sew-in. Deal?" I replied, waiting for her response.

"Oh my God, frannn! Thank you so much! Yes, you know I will do it. Shit, I need the money. I left with nothing but one duffle bag and Ricaria's diaper bag that is here," she whined as she ran her hand over her pixie cut, I had hooked up for her a few months back. Skai had beautiful hair so when she arrived asking for me to fix up the cut, she did I was taken aback but the cut fit her perfectly.

"Cool. She wants the basic *Poetic Justice* braids, and I already told her the price is $150 with the hair. I have a box of hair in the back already that Bilal got off this booster for me. So just go head get yourself cleaned up. Take a sip of some wine and let's get this money. Then we'll go grab some dinner," I said as we hugged each other.

****

It was well after nine o'clock when we both finished up our clients, and we were beat. Ricaria had long been asleep, so I called my brother up and asked him to bring us some food. I took a hot shower and threw on my PINK pajama short set and fuzzy slippers and decided to roll up a blunt while waiting for our food. Skai showered and put on a racerback tank top and biker shorts with some fuzzy UGG slippers I had got her. I was 2 years older than Skai, so I treated her like a little sister and honestly, blood couldn't make us closer. I met Skai when I would do our girl, Gianni's, hair back in the day, and she would tag along. Skai's mother died when she was 14 from breast cancer, leaving her alone, and she ended up in foster care.

Her foster mother was strict as hell on her, and when she lost her virginity to Rico's pedophile ass and ended up pregnant, she tossed her out and reported her as a runaway. I went through the system too, so I had a soft spot for Skai. I took her in until Rico came and collected her up. He'd been controlling her ever since. We both had some rough things happen to us, and I'm just ready for us to heal and do better. With Ricaria watching us, we had to give her a better example. Leaving Buffalo was the best thing we ever did. You best believe when he uprooted my little sis, I was right there. Soon after, my brother and his boys, Avino and Jorah, expanded they business to NYC, and here we all were except for Gianni.

Gianni was still in College for her business degree to go along with her Culinary degree, but she came to visit all the time. Especially with her Auntie Giselle here in the city too. We all tried to get her to transfer schools, but she only had one semester left, and we were kidnapping her ass immediately after. Speaking of her, I needed to see how her vacation in Georgia was going. Just as I was picking up the phone to call Gianni, there was knocking at my door. I loved my girl, but a bihh was starving, so I would hit her first thing in the morning.

I didn't even check the peephole; I just swung the door open to see my longtime crush, Avino, smiling, holding bags of food. Avino was like a Greek god in my eyes. Everything was perfect on him. He had this sun-kissed caramel complexion, the perfect kissable lips, and bright-white straight teeth. He had dreads that hung long past his shoulders. They were nice and neat, thanks to me, his stylist. And his eyes? Whewwww! Them brown eyes was everything and had me gone.

I'd had the biggest crush on Avino since back when I first went to stay with my brother a few years ago. I never let anyone but Skai and Gianni know, and I never acted on it. The way his sexy ass just strolled past me up in my apartment had me ready to let him know, but I was always too nervous he would reject me. Therefore, I never shot my shot at him. He had kicked his Timbs off at the door and was in the kitchen taking food out. I just shook my head because this was normal for him to make himself at home when he came by my spot. I was just about to close the door when my brother and Jorah walked in with more bags, and I knew that my brother had picked me up some groceries. I loved Bilal. He always made sure his sister was straight, even when our parents didn't.

"Bilal, all I asked for was dinner. I just made some good money doing hair. I was going to get groceries tomorrow!" I shouted to his back as he walked into my kitchen. I locked up the door and went to join these knuckleheads.

"Sis don't even worry about it. I appreciate you helping me out last month. I still ain't find nobody with your caliber of skills at whipping up that work, so I may need you again at the end of this month," he said with his sneaky grin plastered on his face.

"I really ain't trying to join your crew, Bilal, but I got you. And you better find someone quick because I'mma be renting a booth at the salon on 125th soon," I said as I pulled out plates and utensils so we could all eat.

I was damn near about to bite my lips off I was so hungry, and the delicious smell of the Jamaican jerk chicken and coconut mango rice was not making it better.

"Sis, with the money you could make working for me, just cooking up for us, you can open your own shop in no time. Fuck working for anyone," Bilal replied as he stuffed a plantain in his mouth.

"Yea, I hear you, big bro. Maybe I will. Just let me think on it," I said as I piled up a plate and sat at my dining room table.

I didn't have a luxury apartment, but it was decent and above a vitamin store, so it was cool for me, and now Skai and Ricaria. I was so busy eating I hadn't paid attention to Jorah, or JD as we called him, and how fascinated with Skai he was. She was at the other end of my rectangle pub-style table stuffing her face as well and laughing in between at what Jorah was saying. I could see the admiration in eyes, and he was feeling my girl, which was cool. Jorah was a good dude. He had been running with my brother for a few years, and he was the youngest of the crew. Just like Skai was in ours. I might have to play matchmaker with these two.

I finished up my food and put my plate in the sink. I grabbed a bottle of water and took it straight to the head while I stood in front of the refrigerator with door open. Once I drank enough, I closed the fridge and was startled by Avino's presence. I was instantly lost in his eyes and damn near on the verge of passing out from holding my breath. He looked me up and down as he licked his lips, and I was sure the crotch of my pajama shorts was soaked. Thank God they were black shorts. I swallowed the lump in my throat and finally took a breath. I went to step around Avino, but he blocked me and grabbed my hand. I was sweating bullets because he never was this affectionate towards me, or maybe I was just tripping, and he was just being friendly and not even thinking about my tomboy ass.

"Brie, baby, my gutta baby. Don't you want to hook your boy up before I slide out of here? I got a little booty call set up with this older chick, and I want my dreads to look fresh," he said as he held my hand, waiting for a response.

See, I told my dumb ass he wasn't thinking about me.

"Ughhh. TMI, Vino. But, yea, I got you. Let me get my supplies and what not, and we can get started," I replied as I pulled my hand back and headed to the hall to retrieve my items I'd need from the closet.

I was lowkey crushed that he always overlooked me. I used to go out my way to get his attention, and it never worked. I jumped at the opportunity to twist his hair whenever he needed, no matter the time or how tired I was because it was the only time, I was able to be close up in his personal space. I loved the way his skin felt against mines when he would remove his shirt and sit down on the floor in between my legs—shirtless skin to skin. I loved the way the Dove cucumber soap smelled on him along with the intoxicating smell of his Mont Blanc Legend cologne. When I returned to my living room, we fell in routine, and I twisted his hair as our conversation just flowed. We had so much in common that talking was always easy.

It was well after four in the morning by the time the guys left my house. Skai had fell asleep long ago on the couch, but once the fellas started clowning her for her loud snoring, I woke her up, and she went in my spare room that had the blow-up bed for her and Ricaria all set up.

I climbed in my queen-sized bed with my abundance of pillows, and as tired as I was a little while ago, I couldn't fall asleep. I just laid in bed thinking about how it would be to be laid up under Avino in this bed right now. I had to let these thoughts go because he wasn't checking for me in no way. Plus, I know if Bilal had a say, it would never happen. He was too overprotective of me and for good reason.

I was never confident in my appearance, and I never felt I had the body of a woman. I was always slim and flat chested, Brie. But as my body started to develop, I noticed the attention I gained. Although it didn't build up confidence in me, it damn sure added to my insecurities. From foster home to foster home, I was bounced around and at damn near every single one I had to deal with problems. The very first one I was treated like a worker and not a child and was punished and beat if I breathed wrong. I got sent to the next one to be starved and left for days alone with multiple other kids and then the absolute worst possible place to go was where I ended up, and that was at the Clancy house.

Living there was my final straw with these foster homes. Mr. Clancy was an alcoholic and an abusive man to Mrs. Clancy. But she did whatever he asked, even allowing him to touch and molest on us. This was where I tried my best to be boyish by doing things, like taping my developing breasts down and wearing baggy clothes, but nothing worked to keep me off his radar. Mr. Clancy would still touch and grope me in the middle of the night in a Tweety Bird night gown because his nasty, old ass never cared. The day he tried to force his shriveled-up penis in my mouth, I bit down hard as hell with all pearly white 32's, and he screamed out in agony as blood squirted out. He fell out in pain, and I hightailed it out of that room and out of the house, never looking back.

Back then, my brother had turned 18 just a month ago and was released from the system. He had an apartment with his best friend, and I was going to be the new roommate because I refused to deal with Mr. Clancy. I was 15, soon to be 16, and I could get a job and still go to school. Maybe even a new school. That night I walked 5 blocks in pajamas and long knee-high socks to my brother's apartment. I prayed the whole way there that he was home and would let me stay with him. When I arrived, my brother and Avino were there and they took me in. The rest was history. I always wondered if my mother was out there looking for us. She had lost her mind behind my no-good father. After the neighbor found out she left town to go look for him, leaving us alone, she called CPS, and we'd been in foster care since then.

I wished I could find her, and I'd tried a lot of times but never could get any information. However, I wouldn't give up. One day, I knew I would find her. I wasn't as angry as Bilal was with her, but I was sad that her mental was so clouded by a man who didn't love her, or take care of his children, that she would leave us behind to chase him. I had a lot of questions for her. Somewhere in my heart, I knew I would get the answers, and they would be from her directly, if God willing.

I was finally free and back at home in the ruff buff. I came home to great news too. I had all the credits I needed and no longer was required to do an internship, so this girl was done and just needed to come back for graduation. I decided I would surprise my Auntie Giselle and my girls, Brie & Skai, and head up to New York for good. I had just packed my last suitcase and sold a bunch of my things to my roommate, Cassie. She was a Junior business major and wanted to keep the off-campus apartment for her and her little sister, who would be graduating high school and coming up to Buffalo to go to school with her.

I gassed up my little Toyota Corolla and hit the road to New York. I knew it was temporary because I wanted to live California eventually, but it was the start of a new journey, and I welcome it with open arms. I had spoken to Giselle this morning. She was just returning from a tattoo expo in Vegas and would be home by the time I arrived. She had no idea I'd be pulling up on her and finally coming to live for a little while, like she begged of me for years. I didn't even give my ex, Wesley, a heads up because he was no good anyways. I was finally done waiting on him to get his shit together. I was heading to New York single and free to do me.

I had a nice amount of money saved up, and once I arrived, I planned to work, hopefully as a chef, until I could open my own restaurant and bakery. My drive was going smooth without having to even stop until I was just reaching the Brooklyn Bridge. I had decided to go straight to Auntie Giselle's after I grabbed something to eat so I could be there to surprise her. I had a spare key that I'd had for years, so I'd be able to get in and get comfortable. I decided to stop at Street Cart for a Gyro and a can of pop. I got in line and ordered and then stood off to the side to wait for my food.

They called my number, and just as I was about to grab my food, a young boy snatched my bag and took off running down Park Ave. I was about to go after him when a guy stepped in and stuck his foot out, tripping the young boy but snatching up my food in the process. The boy rolled around in pain, and the guy who saved my food said a few words before tossing him some cash on the ground beside him. He then headed in my direction. The spring breeze was blowing and the sun shining down had this man looking like a whole snack out here. He was not too far from me but stopped to let a few bikers by before he reached me.

"Here you go, miss lady. I hope you enjoy your food," he said with the sexiest southern accent I had ever heard.

"Thank you so much. I appreciate you for helping me. I'm starving and was literally going to cry if I hadn't gotten my food back," I replied while reaching in my purse for some cash to tip him.

"Don't even worry about it, beautiful. I was a knucklehead once. That's why I looked out for lil' homie and dropped him a few bills to get some food the proper way, and, please. No need to pay me. You have a nice day." He grabbed my hand and kissed it before walking off, leaving me stuck on stupid.

Damn, he was just too fine for words with the tattoos, accent, and them brown eyes. Ummph, ummph! I should have asked for his number or gave him mine. Damn. Oh, well. No need for distractions no way. I had plans, and they didn't include no sexy men that would have my head all the way gone and off track over them. I would not be stupid for a boy never again. After the things Wesley took me through, I would never allow that to happen, so back to my focus and grind.

****

"Surpriseeeeee!" I yelled as soon as Auntie Giselle walked through her door looking like a video vixen in her shades, crop top, leather jacket, and skinny jeans.

"OH MY GOD, GIGI!" she yelled as she dropped her bags and ran over to me in the living room.

We hugged and danced around like kids. Even though she was my aunt and was twelve years older than me, she treated me like a little sister, and I loved it. Especially since I was the only child.

"I just got in today and decided to surprise you. I am actually here to live. I have more than enough credits for graduation in May and no internship required due to my 4.0 GPA." I beamed with pride as I helped bring her bags inside her room.

"Baby girl, I am so proud of you. I am so glad to have you here. You know the spare room is all yours for as long as you need it. I wish I had known you were coming. I would have got you a gift, and I wouldn't have taken Torrian up on his offer for a date tonight," she said as she started to remove items from her bag.

"It's cool, Auntie. I'm here for a while. We have more than enough time to hang. Plus, I'mma slide over to Brie's house and see her and go see Skai and Ricaria, so it's all good. Go enjoy yourself. I will be happy when you and Torrian finally tie the knot. Y'all are so perfect for each other," I said as I laid across her huge California King bed.

"Oh, boy. Not you too. That's all Torrian talks about is when I will become Mrs. Sloan." She smiled as she started to empty the last suitcase.

"Well, I'm team Uncle Tory all day. You know that Auntie," I said as I headed out the room to call up my girls.

I couldn't believe I changed my number on Rico's ass. I knew he was pissed off and was waiting on me to come home, but too bad I wasn't. I was glad I never gave him Brie's new address. Bilal's old apartment was they trap house, so he could pop up over there, and they would beat the brakes off his ass. I was getting my hair finger waved and curled by Brie because we were going out tonight with Bilal, Avino, Jorah, and a few other people. It was JD's birthday and he invited us out, specifically asking me to be his date. I was blushing last night when he dropped that bomb on me, but I gladly accepted. It shocked the hell out of me because I hadn't been with anyone other than Rico, but it was something about Jorah that had me interested.

We shopped earlier and took Ricaria next door to Mrs. Bailey who we adored like a grandmother. She'd gotten her and her granddaughter, Nokia's, hair done by Brie and me a few times over the last year, and she loved her some Ricaria. I had got the call back from the Dance center this morning for the head dance instructor position for the youth classes, and I was on cloud nine. I'd get paid a nice little salary too from the children's classes alone but also from the community center job I accepted teaching dance fitness classes and pole dance classes. I would be bringing home about $1000 a week from both jobs, and it was needed. I would stay with Brie for a few more months while I stacked up the money and then I would find a nice place for me and my princess.

I was looking myself over in the mirror, dressed in a money green tight jersey knit dress and my knee-high money green boots. I paired it with the Fendi multicolored bag that Brie got for the low from this booster chick she had as a client. My hair was styled perfect in my curls and waves with my diamond stud earrings. I was loving the makeup that Brie did. It wasn't too much but just enough. I was going to sit and finish off my glass of wine when the doorbell buzzed.

"I got it, Brie!" I yelled out to her as she finished getting ready.

I checked the peephole, but it was covered up. I instantly got nervous. I asked who it was, but no one said anything. Instead, they knocked again. I wasn't about to open the door because it could be Rico, and I wasn't built today to fight him. Knowing Rico, he would try to kill me. The knocks came again and then I heard a voice that made me breathe easy. Excitement set in as I snatched the door open after unlocking it. And sure enough, there stood Gianni looking like a million bucks.

"OH MY GOD, GIANNI!" I yelled and hugged her tightly.

Gianni was my first and only friend when we grew up on the east side of Buffalo. We used to have sleepovers and hang out all the time until my momma died, and I was shipped away to the south of Buffalo in foster care. When I met Rico, I thought my life would be better, but he just made it a living hell. Gianni kept in touch with me, and we all became the best of friends. More like sisters. I would never forget all that her and Brie did for me and Ricaria over the last year.

"I've missed you girls so much that I packed up everything, got in my car, and came here to live," she said as we finally stopped hugging.

"Wait, what?! You moved here?!" I shouted with excitement.

"Yes, Gianni. The Chef has arrived in the Big Apple. My advisor gave me the green light after he did my review and realized

I had more than enough credits to graduate. My 4.0 GPA meant I didn't have to do an internship, so all that was left to do was go back in a month for graduation," she replied with a huge smile on her face.

"BRIE get out here now! It's important!" I yelled out so Brie could see Gianni and be just as surprised as me.

"What you are yelling for, Skai? I'm almost done. Just trying to find the perfect outfit," she said, coming around the corner in her sports bra and thong.

"The stylist is here to help you miss Brie because that t-shirt dress in your hand is a no-go," Gianni said, stopping Brie in her tracks as she finally looked up and saw who was speaking.

"OH MY GOD, BEST FRANNNNN!" Brie ran to Gianni and hugged her tightly as they did the hop around like we had done moments prior.

"Yes, I am here, and I am here to stay," Gianni said while smiling hard at a confused Brie.

After she told her the same details about school, we all had a few glasses of wine before they started to get ready. Gianni had a suitcase in her trunk with everything she needed. She also was able to makeover Brie because she had the whole sexy tomboy thing going, but now with Gianni's help, she was looking like a grown ass sexy woman out here. We all snapped some pics for the Gram, Facebook, and Snapchat, which was all new to me, but now that I was no longer tied to crazy ass Rico, I was living my best life carefree and loving it.

Gianni was dressed in a sparkly glitter body con dress with the back out and tan tie-up heels, and Brie flat ironed her hair for her. And miss Brie was dressed in a pretty ankle-length black dress that zipped up the front from the thighs to the breasts with pretty black strappy heels. She wore her hair full and curled, and her makeup was beat to the gawds. She looked amazing, and I hoped she would start coming out her shell more. I know she had been through a lot, but she was beautiful, and any man would love the chance to have her if she would just allow them in.

We were seated in VIP awaiting the arrival of the guys and they crew for Jorah's birthday party. A few guys had sent over bottles to our section, and we were getting buzzed but trying to limit it. Especially Skai since she was not a huge drinker, and she wasn't even 21 yet. They started playing all the songs that we could twerk to. Just as we were getting started, in strolled the guys, and I about passed out when I laid eyes on Avino. He looked so good in his white button up shirt and gold chain, dreads hanging, dark blue Levi's and his Wheat Timbs.

I tried to play it cool, but when he hugged us all and pulled me in by the small of my back, I started to feel wobbly and weak in the knees. He kissed my cheek and whispered in my ear, "Damn, Brie, baby. You are looking damn good tonight. I hope you save me a dance," before kissing my neck softly and heading over to where the bottle girls were pouring the drinks in our section.

I threw back the rest of the Remy that was in my glass before grabbing a glass of Champagne that was being passed out so we could toast up and celebrate Jorah's 25th Birthday. We all raised our glasses and then drank. We watched on as the bottle girls sang happy birthday and brought the cake out to JD. He blew out the candles, and we all asked what he wished for.

"I wished for a good woman, and I think my wish was already granted." He never took his eyes off Skai as he spoke.

Skai was blushing and cheesing hard as hell, and I was shocked at how much chemistry was flowing between them. All this time I thought I had to play match maker, and they dun' beat me to the punch. I watched as Jorah made his way over to Skai and pulled her in for a dance. She was working him to the Reggae beat that boomed through the club. Skai was a professional dancer, but club dancing and battle dancing was her calling for real. She always killed it.

I was starting to feel the buzz from the all the drinks, so I decided to go walk out on the balcony that was off our section and catch a breeze. I stepped outside and immediately was stopped in my tracks as I watched this handsome man beat the shit out of another guy. There were a few guys in all black that appeared to be bodyguards of some sort surrounding the fight. I was stuck frozen in place as they finally picked the half-conscious man up and dragged him down the stairs of the balcony to the street. The handsome aggressor of the fight was fixing his clothes and then he looked up into my face. I felt stupid as I just stared at him, not even speaking one word.

"I apologize for that, shorty. I didn't mean to do that in your presence. Balcony is all yours." He stepped around me and walked off into the section next to ours.

The balcony had some standing tables and a few lounge seats, so I took one and enjoyed the breeze. I was relaxing and sobering up, just resting my eyes a little, when I felt someone looking at me. I opened my eyes to see the same guy with two drinks in his hand. He reached one out to me, and I gladly accepted it.

"I felt bad that I acted a fool out here in your presence, beautiful, so I got you a drink. Just a small way to apologize and in hopes you will let me take you out to make up for it?" he said as he sipped from his drink before sitting beside me.

He was built and tall with a beard to die for and had a light skin complexion. He gave off boss vibes. I was enjoying his attention, so I accepted the invite and we continued to talk and chill before exchanging numbers. I hugged him and before he released me, he kissed my cheek and sent electric currents all through me. I waved before walking back to the section to find everyone all boo'd up accept me and Avino. Avino was white boy wasted, and I decided to pull him outside to the Uber I called because he was done.

I woke up smiling and feeling the happiest I could ever remember feeling. Days with Rico, I did not even want to get up out the bed, for fear I'd do something that would send his hand upside my head or across my face. Today, Jorah was the reason for my smile. We had gone out to breakfast last night: me, him, Gianni, and Avino's older brother, Nosaj, who ended up remembering Gianni. Apparently, he stopped some kid from stealing her food on Park Ave. Brie took Avino's drunk ass to her crib to crash and sober up, and Bilal left with his ex, Amerie. Those two were something else—always breaking up to make up and back and forth again. I had a good morning text from Jorah, and I was just about to text him back when Gianni finally strutted her ass in the apartment.

I watched her as she eased in with her heels in one hand and her phone in the other, smiling wide as she responded to a text, I assumed. All the lights were out, and the sun had not fully come up yet, so she attempted to tip toe to the bathroom. However, I flicked the light on fast, scaring the shit out of her. I fell out in a fit of laughter as she began to swing the fuzzy throw pillow at me. I ducked and dodged it and finally collapsed on the sofa. Gianni did the same. I was out of breath and feeling thirsty as ever. I stood to go get water but not before grilling Gianni.

"So, where yo' sneaky ass coming from, Gi?" I asked as I

walked off to get a bottle of water.

"I went for a ride with Nosaj, just kicking it. We actually all have plans with the guys at some paintball range and then a kick-back at the spot for food and drinks," she replied, now grabbing a water as well.

"Oh, yea. I got a text about that from Jorah. Sounds cool. Now what about little miss 'nurse my secret man back to health' in there." I tilted my head towards Brie's room where we could hear her and Avino snoring like crazy.

"Girl, her ass will go just to be around Avino. I will be glad when she admits she is feeling him and let him know'because I know he is feeling her too. It's all in his eyes. He be watching her hard, and he was pissed last night when she was talking to that nigga, Blue, out on the balcony. Quiet as it's kept, Avino probably got drunk on purpose so he could block ole' boy," Gigi replied, laughing, before heading to go shower.

I went and picked up Ricaria from next door at Mrs. Bailey's and spent the rest of the day with her. We watched her favorite shows, played dolls and snacked out. I had arranged to take her back to Mrs. Bailey this evening and even offered to pay her, but she refused and said that Ricaria was her honorary granddaughter. I was thankful for her because she loved us like we all were really her kids. Growing up alone in the foster system and to love a man who turned out to be the biggest fraud of them all, even after all his promises to protect and love me, he failed, but I refused to be bitter behind him. I would be better.

I laid still, awake in my bed, with arms wrapped around me that had me scared to know whose they were. I wasn't that fucked up last night, but liquor did creep up on me sometimes. *Damn, I hoped I didn't do no hoe shit last night. Fuck,* I thought to myself. I slowly rolled onto my back from the spooning position and saw a naked Avino in my bed. I rubbed my eyes to make sure I wasn't dreaming, and sure enough, with ten inches of morning wood, he was here—one leg and his eggplant sticking out the cover. I looked down at myself, and I was still fully clothed. Except my dress was above my waist with no panties on or in sight. I hurried to my bathroom in my room and shut the door, locking it behind me as I started the shower nice and hot.

I stood in the shower and tried to recollect my thoughts of what might have occurred last night. I slowly started to remember meeting Blue and exchanging numbers as well as Avino being shit faced drunk, so I offered to drive him home. I drove his car to my house instead, where I had left him on the blow-up mattress in the room, I gave Ricaria and Skai. So, when did he end up in my bed and naked? Damn, I wish I could remember if we did anything. From the way it looked, we just might have. I started to self-examine my kitty, and it was still tight and untouched. No soreness, which I know once I did decide to bust it open for someone, it was gon' be some pain involved because it'd been so long. I stepped out the shower and pulled my terry cloth robe on, tying it tightly.

I entered my room to find Avino gone and a note on my dresser that read, *Thanks for taking care of your boy. I appreciate you, and I owe for that, for real. Stay sweet baby doll. ONE. P.S. You got lucky.*

I felt all warm inside with butterflies, but I was a bit confused on what he meant by "You got lucky." I know we ain't have sex because I wasn't sore. I'd been celibate for damn near a year now after things ended with Hansim, so I was lost as to what that meant.

I texted Bilal and let him know I was down to work with him and make some money. I had plans to get going and moves to set in action, and with the little money I was making, I could never invest into my business as soon as I would like. I then set up my hair appointments for all day Sunday, leaving today free to do whatever. I also responded to a good morning text from Blue. It was something about him that I really found interesting. He was sexy, mysterious and I could tell he was way older than me.

Maybe after all the bullshit Hansim put me through, he was what I needed. Hansim was my first real boyfriend, and although he wasn't my first, he was the one I loved deeply and stupidly. He played me and robbed me blind, but he got caught up by the police and was now serving a ten-year sentence. So, karma handled him for me.

Enough of his ass, though. It was a minor setback for a major comeback. I made my way to the living room to find Gianni passed out on the couch and Skai and Ricaria playing with dolls. My God-baby jumped up with curly hair swinging as she ran, and she ran right to me. I scooped her up and let her tell me about her day while her mama gave me the side eye with a smirk. I already knew what she was thinking. I ignored the looks and took my God-baby to get our secret snack bag we had hidden in the kitchen with our favorite fruit snacks. As soon as we sat at the dining room table and started eating our snacks, in came Skai storming over to us. She snatched the fruit snacks out my hand, causing some to spill.

"Don't try to act like you ain't got some explaining to do, young lady?" Skai said with her hand on her hip, tapping her little ass foot.

"Girl, if you don't chill out, I'm gon' smack you. Relax, sis. Trust me, nothing happened between us, and he still don't know about my crush on him. Although he did leave me a letter before he left, and it has me a bit confused. But I know we ain't fuck. It's still cobwebs down under and tight as a lock without a key." I laughed as she rolled her eyes and went back to the living room.

Once Gianni was awake, the girls informed me of the plans, and I was down. Plus, I could have Blue come through since he was trying to see me today. We all dressed casually in jeans and fitted tees, or crop tops, and sported our kicks in place of the heels. The guys were already at the paintball park waiting on us. I was a tomboy and always loved playing these types of games and activities, so I couldn't wait to kick these boys' asses. We all hopped in GiGi's car after walking Ricaria to Mrs. Bailey. I was too hyped like a kid at the candy store. This type of stuff was exactly my type of fun.

****

We were all posted up at my brother's house after all the fun we had at the paintball park. I was ducked off on the side of the porch texting with Blue. He asked to see me and take me for a ride, so I gave him the street and cross street that my brother's Brownstone was on to come get me. I headed back inside just to let everyone know I was gon' slide for a quick minute, but I'd be back. I entered the dining area to a rowdy crowd consisting of Bilal, Amerie, Nosaj, and Gigi, while JD and Skai watched on. The couples were in an intense game of Spades, cracking jokes, and arguing back and forth.

Avino had left off on his own after paintball but said he would be over later. I wanted to get some time alone to talk to him about last night, but oh, well. I guess I would see him later.

I let them all know that I would be back and made my way to the porch to watch for blue. He said he would be in a red Aston Martin Vanquish. I had no clue what type of car that was, but I was certain it was expensive. I was halfway up the block when a nice red car with pitch black tints turned the corner. The bass in the car had the ground of West 10th street vibrating. I stopped in my tracks as the car pulled right up to me and Blue hopped out. Leaving the car running in the middle of the street, he crossed over to approach me. I could hear Rick Ross' "Diced Pineapples" blaring through the car. Once he was up on me, I instantly smelled his Yves Saint Laurent Cologne La Nuit De L'homme. The smell was intoxicating and captivating and had me standing like a deer caught in headlights once he reached where I stood.

"Hey, beautiful. You ready?" he said as he licked his lips and grabbed my hand, not giving me a minute to even respond.

With the blink of an eye, he was leading me to the passenger side of his car. My feet just floated as if I was on clouds as I followed behind this smooth, sexy man.

"You got here fast. I'm sorry, I didn't mean to have you searching the block for me," I said as he stepped back to let me in his car. The inside smelled just as good as him, and I sank down into the butter-soft leather seats.

"You good, love. No worries. I'm glad you accepted my date." He smiled before closing the door and jogging around to the driver side. Once inside, he reached in the back and handed me a bouquet of pink roses.

I thanked him, and he winked, pulling off up the street.

We ended up going for dessert at Peter Pan Bakery in Brooklyn where we had all types of pastries and cakes while we talked and laughed. Hanging with Blue was refreshing, and time flew by. He ended up getting an urgent call, so he dropped me back off at my brother's place and we made plans to go to dinner tomorrow night. I was shocked when he got out and pulled me in for a sweet, sensual kiss. I watched him pull off before going up the stairs to be greeted by an angry Avino. He was giving me the death stare as I made my way up the steps.

"Hey, Vino. What's wrong? Why you look like you about to whoop somebody's ass?" I laughed as I waited for him to respond.

"So just like that, you out here kissing niggas and shit?" he spat as he stood to his feet, off the steps.

I had to look around and try to figure out who in the hell this nigga was talking to. I checked my surroundings and wasn't no one else out here but us, but he clearly had me all types of fucked up.

"Who in the hell is you talking to like that?! And better yet, when did it become any concern of yours?!" I yelled back, feeling my blood pressure shoot up.

"You right, Brie Brie, baby. My bad for tripping. Your little young ass is grown and obviously blind or dumb. Either way, I'm good on you, though. Do your thing, baby girl." He spoke through clenched teeth and then he was up and inside the house, not even holding the door for me.

I had to use my spare key to get in the door. I was 38 hot and beyond pissed off. This nigga just blew my high that Blue put me on. I was headed to give him a piece of my mind when I was stopped in my tracks by some water head, purple lace front wearing, broad that was posted up on his lap. This nigga had some nerve to be talking shit to me and yet here he was with a bitch in the house for him. He was about to get a rude awakening if he thought shit was sweet. I was about to fuck shit up and get petty. I'd have to deal with my brother later once I said what was needed to be said with a little embellishment.

I stormed, ignoring everyone asking me what was wrong, and I went right to my target. "So, you just tripped on me for having a nigga drop me off, and you got whole Troll-looking broad sitting up in your face? Tuhh. Nigga, you must be a crack baby trying to play with me. Do this bitch know you was in my bed until eleven this morning butt ass naked with your little shrimp dick out cuddled up?"

He had jumped up and pushed her ass down, snatching me up quick by my arm. But I did not give a fuck. I was ready to play.

"Why you are playing with me, Brie? You do not want to do that. You made this shit clear, even after last night. So, what the fuck you want me to do, huh? Drunk mouths speak a sober mind. Hell, yea I woke up in your bed, and you know damn well my dick ain't little, so stop the games. I would have probably woken up in your bed again, but I am not playing these games with you. You keep me at arm's length and rejected me how you did last night. Keep that same energy, ma. You happy now? Pilar let's roll!" he shouted through clenched teeth, releasing me and brushing past me, dreads swinging wildly.

I couldn't even say shit as everyone stared at me. I felt stupid as hell for how I just reacted. I now knew what his letter he left meant. Here I was, secretly lusting after and wanting him, and he wanted me back, but I shot him down. I didn't even remember turning him down, but a part of me wondered if that was my insecurities or truly because I knew I wasn't ready to cross those lines with Avino again. Yea, I said again because Avino was my first, and for as long as I could remember, I always thought he'd be my only. However, that quickly changed. I was just pushed aside as soon as him and my brother flourished. When they made a name out here, the hoes came flocking. Avino also had his reservations because I was 5 years younger than him and also his best friend's little sister.

I tried calling Avino, but he put my ass on the block list, so my call was rolling right to his voicemail. I left him a message apologizing and asking him to call me back. I was sitting in my brother's spare room, the one I used to occupy, when there was a knock at the door. I got up and opened the door to a pissed off Bilal. I knew my brother would be pissed, but at least I didn't have sex with Avino last night.

"I know, Bilal, you are feeling some way about this, and I'm sorry. But that is just how it is. I'm grown now," I said as I plopped back down on my old full-size day bed.

"Don't speak for me, Brie. You know I hate that shit. I already knew your little hot ass was feeling Avino for a minute, and I read your old diary, so I know you let him be your first. I am not mad anymore. I made sure to torture you for it when I acted broke for a month not giving you stacks of money," he said with a mischievous smirk on his face.

I was shocked and slapped his arm. "I can't believe your

nosy ass knew all this time. Why you never said anything?" I asked as he sat in the computer chair.

"I never said anything because, at first, I was too mad for words. And second, after I pressed Avino about it, he told me his intentions and that he was gon' wait until you were older. That is why he fell back from dealing with you because you were still young, and we were just getting started heavy in the streets. I respected him for that and knew he would always have your back and protect you. I can't tell you what to do or what not to do, but don't play games with that man. He waited patiently to even attempt to start up something on the strength of his love for you and me as his best friend." He kissed my forehead and exited the room.

I needed a nap. I had too much on my mind.

I loved Brie plain and simple, but I could not take rejection or seeing her with another nigga especially right in my face. It took everything in me to not rock that nigga once his lips touched my baby lips and then her waterhead ass let him do it. I was so pissed off I had to shut it down and head into the house before I really spazzed on her. I had this mixie from the strip club slide through with me just because I ain't know where Brie head was at after the night we shared. I was trying to play it cool and keep shit on her terms but that was hard as hell to do when I was really feeling her. Truth be told I was in love with Brie and I always had been. She had been through some shit but that didn't change her beautiful spirit. She was chill and laid back and funny as hell. We just meshed and flowed well.

I wasn't expecting her to come in on shit and I let the cat out the bag out of anger and that ain't like me to have loose lips especially about my own personal shit. But oh well it was time for it to be known. I had been patient for the last two years after her breakup with that nigga Hansim. I had let her slip away when we were younger because I had to much going on and she was too young to be tied up in my shit. I was shocked when she first came in my bed years ago after she moved in with Bilal and me. I was half sleep when she wrapped her small hands around me and slept on my chest. She didn't have a body out of this world, but it was filling in nice and I had taken notice secretly.

That became routine and about three months down the line we took things to a level I never had expected. When she came in this one particular night there was burning passion and sexual tension in the air. I tried to do our norm and play it off, but she wasn't going for that. She stripped out her pajamas and laid in my bed naked as the day she was born. I made love to her breaking her virginity and now owning the lotus flower between her legs. She instantly wanted us to be exclusive, but I couldn't give her that and started to regret going to a physical level. I knew we would be together but not at that time. I tried to explain that to her, but she just shut down on me shut me out and did her own thing.

Brie carried on like nothing happened and I figured that was best, so I let things be and let her live. But make no mistake I was always coming back, and I let her know that all the time, but she tried to ignore me and play the games until today. Now here I am ignoring her ass as she blows my phone up for the 30th time tonight. I wasn't playing with Brie though I was gone let her feel the aftermath a little longer before I snatched her up and tamed her. I was well aware of the feelings she had for me and as much as she tried to hide it and fight it, I know what it is. I let her play long enough and I had some real plans in store for us and I was almost done putting things in order and once I was, I wasn't playing anymore games with her.

I knew I would have to sit down and have a talk with Bilal about everything because I promised him years ago, I would take care of Brie and her heart. After everything she has been through, I knew dam well to not play with her and string her along. I knew once I stepped, I needed to step correct. I decided that the time was approaching so I had to get this street shit all the way under control before I try to make her my wife. Yea a nigga was done chasing and playing with these females out here when I knew I had the right one waiting on me. I couldn't wait to come home to her and know she was not just my girl but my wife and then make her the mother of my kids.

My time with Jorah was everything and then some. He treated me with so much respect, but he also played and flirted with me also making me blush like a schoolgirl. I never thought anyone would ever have interest in me because I allowed Rico's words to make me insecure, but Jorah loved everything about me even my short ass hair and small breast. We had quite a few drinks the other night at the kick back and although we did not have sex things were hot between us. Jorah was laid back and he always kept me laughing until my face hurt. I did not want our night to end but I also did not want to appear as if I was easy or desperate. Coming from a situation like I had come from with Rico caused me to always second guess everything. I wondered if Jorah's intentions were pure or was, he is playing me. Did I have the ability to tell the difference with how broken I am. I did not know if this would be anything more than a friendly encounter, but I wanted to live in the moment and find out.

He wanted to take me out today just him and I on a real date. I had never been anywhere but to the movies or fast food spots with Rico. I was so nervous about it, but I was excited too at the same time. I decided to take Ricaria out to Chuck'E Cheese today and spend some quality time with her first before my date tonight. I decided to go to the location farthest out to avoid running into Rico or any of his crew. I pushed the paranoia and fear of him deep down so that I could enjoy my life. I was taking back all the control and power over my life. I needed to be a better example and role model for my baby girl. She deserved to be raised in a healthy and stable environment even if it was just with me. I thought that she needed her father, but I realize now that being a great single mother was better for my baby than a beaten or even worse dead one behind her no-good father.

No one wanted to roll out with us but after much convincing I got Gigi to tag along. She only agreed because I promised to go to the mall with her afterwards. Brie had hair to do and then a date lined up with Blue. Things had been picking up with them two and my girl seemed happy. I know the past she came from and she just deserves some happiness. Seeing the smile on her face and the shell she had up come down was heartwarming to say the least. I wanted us all to get our happily ever after and things looked to be heading in that direction.

****

I did a once over in the mirror before heading out on my date. I was pleased with my looks and felt a surge of confidence that I was not used to. I avoided mirrors in the past because I didn't want to see the bruises and scars that decorated my body. I hated the haircut when I was forced to first get it and I hated the tomboy body that Rico taunted me for having. I shook all the negative thoughts and memories out of my head and made my way out. Brie was walking past me in the hall on the phone with her hair wrapped up after doing her makeup. I smiled doing a twirl as I showed her my look for the night, and she gave me a smile back with a thumbs up.

When I stepped outside the apartment building Jorah was posted against his truck looking fine as hell. He was built with milk chocolate skin and a full beard. I took my time walking to him, but I guess I was going to slow for him because he met me halfway and pulled me in for a hug. I melted instantly into his arms and the smell of his cologne tickled my nose and awakened my senses. This man was just that a true man and he did something to me every time I was around him.

He finally let go and opened the passenger door for me. I climbed in and reached over to open the door for him, and he just stared at me for a moment before climbing in.

"Why you look at me like that?" I was a bit nervous because maybe I wasn't appealing to him at the moment maybe he no longer saw anything in me.

"I never had a woman reach over and open the door for me. My mama said to me when I get a woman who does that, I have found the one. I think she may be right." He answered and pulled off into traffic not saying anything further just letting the music take over the silence that fell on us.

I was shocked at that answer and pleased at the same time. I prayed that I was making the right decision to follow my gut on pursuing Jorah. I couldn't handle another Rico or any type of variation to what he was. I needed a real man and one who would have patience and understanding with me. I had to be careful of who came into my life because I had Ricaria to think about first and foremost.

"What you deep in thought about over there?" Jorah took my hand into his and intertwined our fingers. Heat radiated between our palms and sent my body temperature up a notch.

"Just surprised at how gentle you are for such a thug. You are really sweet despite the tough exterior you have." I replied while nervousness took over me under his glare.

He didn't respond he just winked at me and kept driving. Riding shotgun in his ride gave me a rush like nothing I felt before and the butterflies swarmed about in my belly. We pulled up to the Karaoke Bar and my smile grew wide. He didn't tell me what all we were doing but he knew through many conversations this was on my to do list. As soon as the car was in park, I was hopping out ready to go in. I reached for his hand and dragged him towards the door. He was cracking up at my hyper ass the whole way inside.

Avino was heavy on my mind today but I fought hard and pushed him to the back of my mind. Avino was with the games and playing with me trying to test me and get me to break down my tough exterior and I wasn't silly I knew exactly what he was doing. I peeped game and now I was moving accordingly. I hadn't been around him since the blow up and between hair and spending time with Blue I was doing ok with that. Things with Blue were going great and getting more serious by the day. Blue made me feel like a woman and I didn't feel like a little girl in eyes how I felt whenever I was with Avino.

I was up early on this Friday packing my bag for my weekend getaway with Blue. He wanted to take me up to the Poconos for this couple's getaway with his friends and their wives and girlfriends. I was nervous because this was all new to me but something about Blue felt right. I packed some sexy pajamas and lingerie just in case things went in that direction. I had no clue what to expect but I welcomed it all. Blue talked to me about my dreams and goals and spoke as if he knew I would be a part of his future. He never made me feel like I was bothering him when I would ask him things or just vent about life to him.

My bell rang and I glanced at the clock on my nightstand and knew it couldn't have been Blue he wasn't due to pick me up for another 2 hours. Skai spent the night with Jorah and Ricaria was with Gigi for the night after her and her new boo Nosaj took his daughter and Ricaria out on a play date. I threw on a robe and raced to the door. I checked the peep hole and closed my eyes and counted to ten. I must have thought him up because right outside my door stood Avino. I took a few deep breaths to calm my nerves and then I pulled the door open partially. I looked at him and he just smirked looking back at me. He held my favorite café's breakfast and a carton of orange juice in hands.

"You gone let me in or do I have to force my way inside?" He replied doing just as he said and pushed his way past me into the apartment.

"You so dam rude ugghh." I slammed the door closed quickly locking it and making my way back to my room to finish packing.

I bent down to pull my shoe storage container out from under my bed when I felt hands on my waist and something stiff on my back side. I jumped up quickly and Avino started laughing at me. I slapped his arm and he fell onto my bad still laughing at me. I tossed a pillow at him and proceeded to finish packing. I tried to hurry and slide all my sexy items in my suitcase, but I wasn't quick enough because Avino snatched the items back out and looked at them with a snarl on his face. I acted as if I didn't know what he was looking at as I started putting my smell goods in the suitcase.

"Wait hold the hell up, where you are going and with who that you need to wear this shit?" Avino asked while pushing the lace thong in my face.

"I am going away for the weekend with a good friend Avino and that's all I need to say about that. Why are you here?" I was nervous under his stare, so I turned back to my suitcase and finished packing.

"Brie I know you not going away with that nigga Blue? You just met that man and you running off for the weekend with him?" He grabbed my arm turning me to face him.

I didn't speak as he stared at me with so much hurt and anger in his eyes. I was tired of waiting in the shadows for him and wishing he would take me and my love serious. Today I was heading on this trip with Blue to finally move past this shit with Avino. The games the up and down emotions I was putting an end to it all. Blue had shown me what it was like to have a man take you seriously and I wasn't missing out on my opportunity to find a love to call my own. No doubts or reservations on where I stood in a man's life. I snatched away from Avino and he just shook his head at me before walking out the door.

I fought the urge to go after him. The front door slammed, I shook my head and rolled my eyes at the bull I found myself in with this man that wasn't mine. I checked my phone to see I was short on time. I hopped in the shower and got dressed just in time. Blue was parked out front on time as he said he would be. He came in and helped take my things to his car. I locked up and stopped by Ms. Bailey's and let her know I was gone. I left a spare key with her in case Skai or Gigi needed it. She also said she would check my mail for me and place it the apartment for me.

****

The ride to the cabins was fun and entertaining to say the least. After Blue drove to his friend's place, we rode on a party bus with the other couples and the few single guys who tagged along. The guys were cracking jokes and having roast sessions the whole way there. The ladies were cool and easy going and I was happy about that. Some females don't like to be friendly to the newcomers, but these ladies were different. I bonded mostly with Shea I assume because we were close in age and had a few things in common. Bridge was her man of 4 years and Blue's right-hand man. Bridge's cousin Griff and his wife Satin were the other couple with us. Stokes, Otto and JL were the single ones in attendance.

Blue made sure to include me in the conversations and didn't leave me feeling left out. The vibe we had going was good and I had pushed the guilt of how things had ended with Avino out my head. I had a few texts from my girls telling me to have fun and let loose. My brother text me telling me to be safe and that we needed to talk when I returned. Bilal was overprotective so I knew he wanted to know about Blue and to be honest he probably already did a check into who Blue was. I just hit him with an ok and told him I loved him and would see him when I got back. Skai told me she was still at Jorah's house and that ricaria was on her way over to spend the day out with them and his son.

As soon as I put my phone away from responding to the messages we were pulling up to the resort. We had one huge private Cabin with an indoor pool and hot tub. The guys took all our bags in and we gave ourselves a tour. Blue had called me over to a room off towards the pool. I left the ladies in the theater room and made my way to where he stood waiting with our bags. I smiled at him as he gave me a lustful stare. I put a little pep in my step getting to him and he sat the bags down pulling me once I was close enough to him. I melted into his arms as he held me around my back tightly. I looked into his eyes and I liked what I saw in them.

"I'm glad you accepted my invite. I love having you around." He placed a kiss to my cheek and let me go. He opened the door and my mouth dropped seeing the massive room with the huge picture windows overlooking the resort. The view was amazingly breathtaking, and I knew I'd get some alone time to sit and look out of it.

"Thank you so much for inviting me. I needed a getaway, and this is just the type of place I needed to come to." I placed a kiss to his cheek, but he quickly grabbed my face and kissed me deeply. I was a bit taken aback but the sparks had erupted, and I melted into him yet again lips locked together. His hands trailed my body sensually and the body heat radiated between us. Blue had backed me into the wall, and I was sure we were about to take things to another level but a few loud knocks at the door rook us out of our zone. I wiped my gloss off his lips as he shook his head. He was debating on ignoring the door, but the knocks came again and we both erupted into laughter when Griff started singing for us to come on out.

I couldn't believe what I saw in Brie's bag earlier. That shit burned me up so bad I was ready to trash all that shit and shut the trip down but I had created this dynamic and I had a few more moves to make and shit to get lined up before I would be ready to give her my all. I never wanted to half step with Brie. I knew the woman she was, and I needed to set us up to prosper and not fail. I was thinking of the future because she was my future and I wanted our shit to be solid with no bull shit in the way. I was starting to think I went about this shit the wrong way. I knew she wouldn't listen to me, so I had to be a snitch and call Bilal on this one and I didn't give a dam. I didn't trust this nigga Blue and he gave off snake vibes, so I was about to dig up the dirt on him asap.

Bilal was pissed off, but he also was clowning me for how I was going behind Brie and she wasn't even my woman yet. He can kill all that noise because she has always been mine and will always be mine. Brie was stubborn as hell and wanted to be the one in control and miss independent and I needed her to realize as a man I was gone lead us and never stop her from being her own woman and boss but she had to let me be the man and run shit especially at home. My plan was to provide and support her dreams. I had my eyes a spot for her to have a hair salon and nail bar. I would invest in it and we would be good to go. I had other business ventures but that was one I wanted to start on first.

I was sick thinking this nigga was touching on my girl and I was ready to go harass Skai for they whereabouts. I knew I couldn't do that without starting up unnecessary beef with Blue. I told myself that in due time I'd have Brie where she belonged and that was with my last name and carrying my baby. I pulled up to the warehouse so I could run the daily count. Things had kicked off for us and now we had a pill supplier as well. Nassir knight was retired but he knew Bilal well and always tried to pull him on his team back in the day. When Bilal reached out Nassir hooked us up with his next in command Remo and we been in business rocking it just us 4 Bilal, Jorah, Nosaj and myself. We sometimes would take the help the girls would offer from time to time when they needed to make some money, but Bilal hated involving them in the game.

I hopped out and headed around back to the secured entrance. I was greeted by our only security guard Big Fred and we dapped it up before I stepped inside. I stepped into the cold warehouse and flicked on the light switch. I immediately retrieved the duffle bags of money and started up the machines. I turned on my beats pill and let Mobb Deep play as I got to work. I hadn't even heard Nosaj and Bilal come in until they tossed some more duffle bags on the table in front of me. I shook my head because we were bringing in more money than we imagined we would and we didn't rock with too many people to bring them into the fold completely but from the looks of it we needed to recruit a few more soldiers and asap.

"I know you probably don't want to hear this bro, but Gigi was on the phone in the car with Brie before I dropped her off and shorty plan on giving that nigga some cutty." Nosaj shook his head while I took in what he said.

"I ain't even hearing that shit right now bro so let's drop it I just got my mind back focus on the money when I got here, and I want to keep it on that so we can re-up tomorrow. At the end of the day Brie is grown and not my woman right now. I'm a let her rock for now but I'm shutting all that shit down as soon I finish lining everything up." I place the rubber bands on the stacks I was done counting and everyone else let the topic go and followed suit and started counting the money up with me.

I was lowkey crushed hearing that, but I kept that shit to myself. It was a L I had to take for the bigger picture. It gets greater later is how I was looking at it but deep down I was worried that Brie might really fall for this nigga and leave me in the dust. I took my phone out and contemplated texting her, but my ego and pride wouldn't allow me to show her that I was bothered about this shit. I had too much to handle and I couldn't even give her the time and effort she deserved from a man, so I had to let her make her choice and hope that in the end it was me and her.

I stirred out of my sleep and slowly opened my eyes to take in my surroundings. I was so used to sleeping with one eye opened or being awakened from a slap to the face that it was refreshing to get up on my own with no fear of what I would be waking up to. I closed my eyes tightly as a vision came to me from the time Rico snatched me out the bed in the middle of the night by my hair. He dragged me through the house until we reached the patio where he threatened to throw me over if I ever tried to leave him again. That was the first time I had attempted to leave, and it was almost a year ago now. I shook the thoughts away as I sat up fully on the couch and noticed that Ricaria and Josiah were still both fast asleep and Jorah was nowhere to be found.

I went in search of him through his 3-story brownstone. I started on the first level and located him on his back porch smoking a blunt. I didn't open the door right away I just admired him, and his aura soothed me. I was out of my element, but it felt good. Jorah was a breath of fresh air and he was never aggressive or dismissive to me as Rico had been. I realized now how naïve I was to think the mean and aggressive nature of Rico was ok from the beginning. I had all the signs and red flags and I now knew he was never good and never meant me well. I vowed to never allow a man to take me through those things. I was still fragile, and my heart wasn't fully repaired but Jorah was determined still to have it and I was willing to give him that.

He had joint custody of his 5-year-old son, and I had to somehow get full custody Ricaria before Rico could try to come in and take her from me. Rico didn't care at all about her but to hurt me and be vindictive he would try to take her in an attempt to force my hand at coming back to him. He was sick and malicious, and I had to keep him away from her. I finally slid the door open and stepped out onto the back porch. The cool breeze sent a chill down my spine as I inhaled the smell of his Kush mixed with the city grit. He looked back at me and gave me a smile before extending the blunt to me. I declined and took a seat in the patio chair next to him. He leaned over and grabbed my hand lifting it to lips and kissing the back of my hand gently.

I was putty in his strong hands as I melted from the simple yet endearing gesture. This man was more than I could have imagined he would be behind the street persona and thugged out exterior. He cleaned up well and had the book and street smarts needed to succeed in the game he was tangled in. Jorah was wise beyond his years and a true gentleman. I prayed it was as genuine and real as it felt because I was falling, falling fast and hard for this man and I didn't want to regret it. I gazed at him with so much admiration because I had poured all my issues and baggage out to him expecting him to flee once I finished the final word of admission. To my surprise he stayed and welcomed the challenge I was.

"How did you sleep?" His deep baritone broke my trance and I smiled at him.

"I slept pretty well actually. For the first time in a very long time I was able to sleep peacefully with no fear of what I would wake up to or be woken up out sleep to a punch slap or scolding hot water." My eyes were getting teary and my voice was shaky as I spoke. I didn't want to put a damper on the mood, but I felt so comfortable with Jorah that I spoke freely about my past and what I endured. The way he gave me his undivided attention was therapeutic for me in some way.

"You don't have to hold that shit in May. I want you to get it out so we can move forward. You need to heal and whatever you need to do involving me listening or whatever I'm here. I'm not going anywhere and as I piece back your shattered heart; I want you to be able to trust that I got you and lil mama. This shit moved quickly but I ain't running from I'm embracing that shit and riding with you ten toes down Skai." His words pierced through me like a pin pooping a balloon. He had broken that last balloon of reservation and doubt and I was all in at this point it was no point in fronting as if I wasn't.

I wiped the tears that tried to escape away and stood to my feet. I placed a kiss to his forehead and headed in to make breakfast. I heard him loud and clear and I wasn't running from anything anymore. My past, my pain or the developing feelings were a part of me, and I would embrace it and grow from it through it and for it. The kids were still sleep when I entered the kitchen. I pulled out everything I needed to start cooking and got right to it. Jorah came in and peaked in on the kids before making his way to the stairs. Just as he was headed up the doorbell rang, and he turned on his feet right back down the stairs to the foyer. He peeked out the side windowpane and dropped his head shaking it before he reached for the doorknob. He turned to me and gave me a pleading look before swinging the door open.

A tall modelesque woman came barging in the home looking about wildly. She stopped in her tracks when her eyes met mine and I gave a faint smile. She rolled her eyes apparently displeased with my presence and turned on her stilettos to face Jorah. He ran his hand down his face in frustration and looked at the clock on the wall. My eyes followed and it was 9 am in the morning. She pointed her long-curved nail in his face with her other hand propped up on her hip.

"Jorah DeLano Simmons, I know that better be a hired chef or nanny and not no bitch you are fucking around my son. I specifically told you the rules and I hear from my homegirl you had my son out with a bitch and her child at the movies and shit like a big happy family." Her voiced echoed through the house and the children stirred up out of their sleep on the couch. Ricaria popped up first and rubbed her eyes as her head turned about quickly until she saw me. She hopped down and raced over to me in the kitchen. I picked her up and Jorah's baby mother gave me the death stare with her mouth slightly agape. Before she could start again Jorah grabbed her by her arm and led her out on the front porch pulling the door closed behind him.

I crossed my arms and leaned against the door as Lacy paced back and forth on the porch huffing and puffing like the little dragon that could. I was the least bit bothered by her theatrics because she didn't hold any weight when it came to my son. She tried to demand shit that she couldn't and shouldn't demand because she was bitter and spiteful. She didn't want anyone to have me if she couldn't. She was intent on making things hard and that was only going to end bad for her. With all the ammo I had I could easily strip my son from her life completely but I wasn't a heartless nigga and I grew up fatherless and I never wanted my child to not have both of his parents so I played fair but this was the shit that was gone have re thinking that decision.

She was still running off at the mouth acting like Evette from Baby Boy when she caught Jody cheating, but the difference was, I wasn't her man and I could see whoever I chose with no worries. Lacy had the chance to be mine when I was just a lookout boy, I pursued her, and she rocked with me in the beginning. As time went on and she was sick of the low level and struggle life I was leading she dipped off and only popped back up when the feds stripped her and her Kingpin boyfriend of everything. She told me that Josiah was in fact my son after 2 years of him being raised by another man she shows up with that story. I don't hit women but that was the first time I was itching to knock her head off.

I had at one time loved lacy and she broke my heart and then she did me and my son dirty. I got a DNA test and a lawyer and now here we are 3 years later and her failed attempts to get me back have resulted to these immature ass tactics she is pulling. I cleared my throat interrupting her rant and she stopped like a dear in headlights and narrowed her eyes at me. I took a moment to gather my words and calm myself, so I didn't come off as an asshole because at the end of the day she was the mother of my child.

"Listen to me Lacy and listen to me fully. I will not play these kid games with you. I ain't your man and it's been that way for years shit before I even knew about Josiah. I could have took everything I had on you and your dumb ass ex and took Josiah from you and trust I still have that info and if you keep playing with me I will use that shit and that ain't a threat Ma it's a promise. You passed up a real one chasing material shit and you fell flat on your ass. I pay child support and take care of my son. I would never have him around someone I didn't trust other than you and that's because you birthed him. Take your miserable ass on home and I will drop him off next week as normal." I didn't allow her to speak as she stood flabbergasted her mouth agape and eyes still narrowed at me, I chucked her the deuces and headed back inside. I slammed and locked the door and headed back upstairs to shower like I had started to do before she arrived.

I knew lacy though and she wasn't done bringing drama to me and my home. She was going to try to run Skai off as she had done the others but Skai was different and I wasn't allowing her to interfere this time. I grabbed my phone off the nightstand as I headed into my master bathroom. I turned the Bluetooth speaker in my bathroom on and connected my phone turning on my playlist. I responded to a few messages from Avino and Bilal about our meeting tonight. I would spend the rest of the day with Skai and the kids and then head out to take care of business and then I'd be right back in the house with them. I hoped that I could convince Skai to stay another night with me. Although we only snuggled up on the couch the feeling I got in my chest as she slept next to me our bodies awkwardly tangled together on the sectional, I enjoyed it.

I came downstairs feeling like a new man after that shower. I let the stress that Lacy tried to put on me run down the drain. The delicious smell of the breakfast that Skai prepared hit my nose and my stomach growled letting me know that I was indeed hungry. I stepped into the kitchen and smiled at the sight before me. Skai was seated at the table with the kids enthralled in a deep conversation about SpongeBob. I wasn't a soft nigga but that touched me to the core to see a woman be so endearing and welcoming to my son. Skai was a keeper and she kept proving that to me over and over again. She was different than these materialistic gold diggers out here and I was lucky to get the opportunity to even share a moment with her let alone the many I had over the last few months. Yea I wasn't letting her go for no one and I promised that.

Prior to Nosaj a love life had been the least of my worries especially after the way my last relationship was. But with him it was effortless, and I was in complete bliss with the time I had shared with Nosaj thus far. I had talked my auntie's ear off so much about Nosaj that I had to bring him to meet her and Torrian tonight. I wasn't nervous about it thought because auntie was cool and if I received her approval of Nosaj I'd allow this whatever it was that was forming between us to continue. For the first time I didn't question the intentions of a man and that felt so good. I spent a lot of time stressing over what men truly wanted from me because of what I seen my mother go through.

I text my girls to check on them because they were both out with the new guys in their lives. Skai was coming out of her shell and I loved this side of her. I warned about Rico long before they had Ricaria, but she was young and in love. I didn't want her to end up like my mother or worse. I didn't take no type of domestic violence from a man it wasn't ok, and it wasn't healthy. I can't say love won't hurt or relationships won't go through things, but never will it be that type of hurt. Jealousy and possessiveness were signs to look for and I saw it in Rico from day one. To know she made it out from under him makes my heart swell. Jorah is good for her I hope they blossom. I like the things I hear from Brie about Blue, but I still feel like in my heart her and Avino are just meant to be.

Avino called Nosaj last night while we were leaving bowling and he was pissed with Brie. Avino loves that girl but he wants to do right by her, so he says. I get the whole not wanting to be in the streets and have her wrapped in anything, but he can't expect her to wait forever for him to be ready. Brie has loved him since we were teens and she obviously isn't waiting anymore. That's a love story I hopes comes true. This blue guy is going to have a hard time with Avino though because he isn't playing about Brie and if he had it his way, he would be up there dragging her ass home. I refused to tell him where she was, but he definitely asked me to drop the location. I couldn't break the G-Code so that was a L he had to take like a man who dropped the ball and underestimated his girl.

I was busy cleaning while auntie cooked most of the meal. She took Nosaj into consideration having me ask him what his favorite meal was. She was prepping for oxtails rice and gravy, greens and cornbread. I would help and do the turtle cheesecake for dessert. I set the dining room table and made my way into the kitchen to help. I let the sounds of Ari Lennox get me in the mood and I whipped about the kitchen like the chef that I was. I loved the fancy dishes I knew to make but these type of comfort and soul meals were my favorite ones to prepare. By the time we finished we had just enough to get ready before the men arrived.

I hurried to the guest bathroom that had now become mines and turned on the shower. I co-washed my natural curls before hopping out the shower. I rushed around the room drying off and pulling out an outfit. I settled on some skinny jeans and an off the shoulder ruffled top. Since we were inside, I slid on my fluffy Ugg flip flops and sprayed on some DKNY Be Delicious. I applied a light coat of lip glass and fluffed my air-dried curls before stepping out the room and into the hallway I bumped right into Auntie Giselle and she looked beautiful in a sleeveless turtleneck top and high waisted jean. She had the same idea and placed her fluffy Ugg slippers on her feet.

I let Auntie go by me first and I headed to open the bottle

of chilled wine. The doorbell chimed and I checked myself in the mirror that hung above the glass console table by the door to check myself out. I placed my eye to peephole and smiled wide when I laid my eye on Nosaj. I opened the door and held two huge Bouquets of roses in his hands. He stepped inside kissing my cheek and I inhaled his cologne and closed my eyes savoring the smell of him. I had closed the door, but a quick knock had come before I could lock it. I pulled it opened and was greeted by Torrian who held a bottle of Champagne and a box of Auntie's favorite chocolate covered strawberries.

We sat around the table after the introductions were out the way and the guys had already begun the sports and politics talking. We passed around the dishes making our plates before saying grace and digging in. The dinner flowed smoothly right into dessert and champagne. Torrian wanted to take Auntie out dancing so they left us two and were on their way. Nosaj helped me clear the table and put the food away. I grabbed our glass and the champagne and made my way to the living room. It wasn't fully spring yet and the weather was still fickle, so I started up the fireplace. I sat on the loveseat while Nosaj sat on the other side of the room on the sofa. He watched me as I scrolled through Netflix.

I tried to appear unmoved, but he was making me nervous the way he was watching me so closely. I settled on Sextuplets and got comfortable. Nosaj got up and came and sat right next to me putting his arm around me leaning back into the loveseat getting comfortable. I laughed and looked up at him. He stared down into my eyes and the way he looked into my eyes sent a bolt of electricity through me. I felt good next to this man and looking into his brown eyes I saw potential. He smirked at me and leaned across me to grab the champagne off the end table. My breath was caught in my throat with how close he was up on me. The invasion of my personal space was sending my mind into another place. Palms were sweating as he pulled back brushing past my breast causing my nipples to harden.

I needed to stretch and put some space between us because I was getting hot and bothered. The weeks were flying by and the more time I spent around Nosaj the less I was able to fight my urges to pounce on him. Nosaj was so dam fine and his laid-back demeanor enticed me. I excused myself quickly stepping over his long legs and heading into the bathroom. I closed the door quickly and held the Marble countertop that housed the sink. I turned the water on splashing a little water on my face to calm my hot ass down. I was a ball of nerves and it showed all over my flushed face. I took a few deep breaths and wiped my face. I stepped back out and bumped right into Nosaj's defined chest and abs.

I looked up into his face and saw the pure lust and yearning in his eyes. He pulled me into him by the small of my back. The palms of my hands kept a small gap between us as they pressed firmly into his chest. Without warning he bent down and kissed me sensually. My firm palms melted, and I closed the gap between us throwing my hands around his neck. He pushed into me and our tongues did a sloppy tango. A stifled moan escaped my lips and he kissed me deeper. He pulled back and stared at me hard before speaking.

"Where is your room?" He asked kissing my neck and un-buttoning my jeans.

"Down the hall on the left." I moaned as his fingers worked my throbbing clit. He kissed me again while walking me backwards to my room. It was no turning back and I was content with that. We were both grown and feeling each other, and I had held out for a while now. Tonight, I wanted to feel him. Needed to feel him and curb these temptations.

I watched from the side of the room as Blue played Pool with his boys. The other ladies were busy catching angles for Snapchat and Instagram. There was a mystery within Blue that I could sense but couldn't figure it out. Last night he seemed to real to be true the way he handled me. He never pressed me for sex last night and instead he just spooned with me until we fell asleep in each other's arms. He gave me space and privacy this morning before we hit the different activities on the resort and now as we sat in the bar, I was feeling the few drinks I'd consumed, and glad Blue was focused on something other than flirting with me. If I allowed the liquor to take over, we'd be fucking before the night was over.

I got up to get a water so I could try to sober up some because I didn't want to cross the line with Blue even though my body was trying to betray my mind with that decision. I ordered my water and took a seat. I felt a presence and turned to face a handsome but nerdy looking gentleman. He smiled and took the stool next to me at the bar. I turned my attention to the water that the Bartender had sat in front of me. I scanned the room avoiding eye contact with him. He leaned over whispering in my ear and I pushed him back with my elbow. He snatched my arm and glared down at me menacingly. My voice was caught in my throat as I tried to get out of his grasp. He started to laugh an evil laugh in my face and finally he released my arm roughly causing my water to spill all over me and the bar top.

I jumped up and stepped back as water dripped off the bar and I went to charge at him, but Blue had beat me to the punch literally. Blue hit the man swiftly with a right and doubled up with a left blow to his ribs sending the man down instantly. Blue commenced to stomping the ma n with black construction timbs. I tried to pull Blue off him, but he swung me off him sending me flying into the bar stool. My back landed into the legs of the stool and I instantly felt like my back was on fire. Tears poured out my eyes as I watched Blue beat the man dam near to death in pure rage. The ladies helped me up and the guys pulled Blue off the man and out of the Bar back to the Cabin. I winced in pain as the ladies helped me to my feet.

The cabin was quiet when we entered and the guys were all seated in the living room with the TV on ESPN, but it was muted as they rotated blunts around. I made my way quickly to the room and stripped the wet clothes from my body heading straight to the shower. I was confused about how I felt because although I appreciated the help that Blue offered with that crazed man, I didn't like the rage that came from him and how he ignored the way he flung me to the floor like a rag doll. He never stopped to check on me and didn't acknowledge me after the fact. The look in his eyes was dark and deadly and it sent a strong chill down my spine making goosebumps pop up all over. I was tempted to call Bilal and ask him to take that road trip and pick me up.

The hot water against my body felt like heaven as the stress rinsed off me and down the drain. I turned the waterfall shower head off and just stood in the steam collecting my thoughts and debating on my next move. I opened the glass door and Blue stood with a huge towel outstretched for me. I tensed because I was naked and had not shown him or anyone outside of Avino my body. He must have sensed my insecurity because he approached me wrapping me in the towel and kissing my forehead. The fear I had not too long ago had passed and security had taken its place which was strange considering the situation He led me to the room and began to dry my body while admiring me. I still had the insecurity on my shoulders but the way his hands moved across my bare flesh helped erase it little by little.

"Dam shorty I'm sorry about that shit earlier. I didn't like the way he handled you. This the second time you done seen a nigga get out of character. I'm a make sure I'm on my best behavior from here on out. You gone let me prove it to you Brie?" He rubbed the raw shea butter up my thighs as he sat on the edge of bed with me standing in front of him.

"I appreciate you having my back with that guy. Just don't go killing someone over something like that. I'll let you prove it Blue." I threw caution to the wind and kissed him.

He pulled me into his lap, and I straddled him on the bed. It had been a long time for me but something in me wanted this. The towel fell completely off, and his hands roamed all over me lighting my body on fire. He lifted up holding onto me and placing me in the bed. He kissed me deeply before trailing licks and kisses down my neck and torso. He spread my legs apart and let out a whistle shaking his head as we stared at each other.

"Dam You glistening like that for me baby?" He rubbed circular strokes on my clit as he stared down at me with lust filled eyes.

I let a few moans escape my mouth and he seemed to take that as his motivation to apply more pressure. The feeling he was giving me just from his touch had my head spinning and my body felt like I was floating. He latched onto my clit and my stomach tightened as I grinded into his face feeling like I would release any minute. Blue slow stroked me with his two fingers deep within my folds while lapping circles on my clit sending me over the edge and I knew the others heard my loud moans of pure ecstasy. Blue got off the bed and stripped out his clothes. He pulled a condom out from his pants placing it on and climbing into the bed and in between my legs.

Work at the dance center and community center was like a dream come true. Working alongside some of the hottest dancers from YouTube and all over NYC was the best thing to me. I had just wrapped up a teen hip hop class and was closing to leave. Jorah refused to let me walk the few blocks to Brie's or take a uber or train to his home in Fort Green. Faithfully around the clock he was out front waiting on me. I locked up and headed out the community center and onto the street. Jorah hopped out to come open my door and before he could reach me Rico appeared from around the side of the building. He ran up on me snatching me up by my neck cutting off my air supply in the process.

"Bitch I been looking high and low for your baldheaded ass. Where the fuck is my daughter?" Spit flew freely as he yelled at me.

I struggled to breathe, and I clawed at his hands trying desperately to get free. Rico's hands loosened and then I was dropped to the grown abruptly. I gasped for air while trying to use the car to help lift myself up off the pavement. When I finally got myself up and together Jorah was stomping Rico out and onlookers stood about filming it. I pulled at him and he finally eased back breathing hard chest heaving up and down. He stormed over to his truck and snatched the passenger door open. He yelled for me to get in the car and I quickly hopped in. He slammed the door shut causing me to jump at the impact of the door slamming shaking the car. He stormed back over to Rico and lifted him up by his shirt and spoke to him while pointing at the truck to me.

Jorah dropped Rico back down to the pavement and Rico rolled around in pain. He looked up with swollen bloody eyes and our eyes locked. I shut my eyes quickly and the truck took off into traffic. I finally released the breath I was holding because I was away from him, but I wasn't sure for how long. Rico was relentless, and he was going to be a problem. I had to get rid of him once and for all. I looked to Jorah and I could see from how tight his jaw was clenched that he was pissed. We didn't speak a word as he pulled up to Brie's place. I didn't want to leave things on bad terms, so I decided to break the ice.

"Thank you for helping me back there. I'm sorry about that." I looked down at my broken nails.

"Don't apologize for that clown. Skai I need you to understand that if your baby father come around again or try this shit again that he did tonight I'm a handle him and it won't be an ass whooping the next time." He lifted my head by my chin and made me look him in his eyes. I saw the seriousness in his gaze. Jorah kissed me deeply and then climbed out.

He opened my door and watched me go inside before he hopped in and pulled off. I walked in to Blue and Brie sitting in the living room on the couch watching TV. I tried to hold my composure, but the cries escaped me quicker than I expected them too. I ran to the bathroom and slammed the door shut resting my head against it as the cries kept coming. Brie banged on the door asking me to open up. I unlocked the door and stepped back as she barged in looking me over from head to toe.

"Skai what is wrong with you?" Brie pulled me in for a hug. I broke down and let all the stress and frustration out on her shoulders.

"Rico attacked me outside work tonight." I pulled back and wiped my face off.

"OH MY GOD. How the hell did he find you?" Brie screamed out quickly catching herself and lowering her voice.

"I don't know Brie. If Jorah hadn't been out there, I would be dead right now. I know it because the devil himself stared me in the face as Rico tried to squeeze the life from me. The way Rico looked at me as he choked me scared the shit out of me. I'm going to have to kill him because after the way Jorah beat his ass, I know he will be back for me." I shook my head fighting the tears that threatened to fall.

"Thank god Jorah was there. Listen you need to go file a restraining order and let the police know everything Skai. Do it for Ricaria." Brie hugged me and left out the bathroom.

I stared at myself in the mirror and examined the way I looked. I refuse to go back to that scared girl I was with Rico. I wouldn't let him break me back down after all it took for me to get to this point in my life. I rebuilt my self-esteem with the help of Jorah too I knew my worth and it wasn't a controlled and abused girl. I gathered myself and went into the room I shared with Ricaria. She was sound asleep in the middle of the bed. I climbed into the bed and snuggled up with her. Staring at her face and stroking her curly ponytails I knew I would kill Rico to ensure our safety. There were no other options for me, and I was coming to grips with that. I wasn't a killer in the least bit, but I had to protect my daughter and myself.

I sat in the cut at the back of the bar with my fitted pulled down low over my eyes watching Blue and his crew. Bilal had got some info on Blue and I was just scoping him out to see what this nigga really be up to. He wasn't from the City and he thought he could come in and start doing as he pleased around here but he was sadly mistaken. Bilal had connections in a lot of states, so he followed through on the info and found out that Blue was a grimy ass nigga that got ran up out of Philly. Blue rubbed me the wrong way and hearing this confirmed the vibe I was getting from him all along. Brie was naïve and more so than anything she wanted to prove a point to me. I knew she was a catch and could find another nigga and although I didn't want that I wouldn't stand in her way of experiencing life.

I was coming back for her when the time was right but that wasn't right now. Regardless of her and I not being official I would never let her fall victim to a lame like Blue so behind her back I was gone get this nigga out the way and out her life. His crew was just as lame as him and they were stupid to be following behind a snitch who got ran out his own city. I never trusted anyone who came to another city and wasn't humble. He was out here cocky like he was that nigga and all the while he was just a sucka ass nigga who had to leave home by force. When we all jumped ship from Buffalo to NYC, we came here humble as fuck and happy for a fresh start. We grinded out and got put on by the HNIC of Brook-lyn.

I would never move how flashy and corny Blue be moving and his whole vibe screams fraud. He was in the bar showing out and being loud bringing attention to himself when a boss that's official would never need to do that. The bitches gone flock off gp, and the niggas gone respect you from your presence alone. I threw back my shot and made my way out the bar. I had enough info and saw enough to know this nigga wasn't a huge threat and any heat we brought his way would probably be welcomed by many. I had heard he was linked to Nassir and Remo in some way, so I shot Remo a text to meet up. Before I made any moves, I wanted to run shit past them first. I had mad respect for Nassir or Knight as the hood knows him. He was retired being a husband and father and I respected that but he's not too far away to still have his hand on shit.

Remo had taken over for Nassir and that's how we got put on. I was in this shit for a short time and I let Remo know from day one I had plans to be legit and this was a temporary means to an end. Bilal was being groomed to be the next lieutenant while Jorah was riding with Bilal, he had some business plans as well. I drove to the diner that Remo said pull up on him at and I shot Bilal a text letting him know as well. Jorah was playing real husbands of Brooklyn and shit out at the movies with Skai her baby girl and his son. I wasn't knocking him at all and let him know that Skai was a good look, but Rico was going to be a problem fo sho. Rico got his ass stomped out by me and Bilal a few times back in the day, so I know this isn't the last that Jorah seen of him.

I walked into the lowkey lounge and immediately saw Remo and a group of cats throwing darts in the back. I headed straight that way stopping to slap up a few people I knew and hug a few of the ladies that stopped me. I stepped up into the section and the Kush hit me instantly. I slapped up each one of them and Remo introduced Aasim Nassir's brother and me. I took a seat on the stool as they talked, they shit about their wives and kids and I just played the cut until they finished up. Drinks and blunts were in rotation and Remo finally took a seat beside me after a few hours. We took back shots of D'Usse and then I started to run down the details of my call for this meet up.

"First I'm a thank you for being a man and coming to me first before acting on this shit. Blue not a part of the camp but he is working off a hefty debt he owes to me so that's the only connection we have. The nigga lost some of my product and cash chasing behind some chick who was leaving him. He a clown to be honest but to keep me from murking his ass he is working for free." Remo stated and threw another shot back.

"He done pooled the wool over my shorty eyes and got her head in the clouds right now, but I don't trust his snake ass and the shit y'all saying about him only confirms the way I been feeling wasn't no jealousy." I blew out in frustration.

"Man, you need to get your girl from up under him he can't be trusted, and he known for doing fuck shit to females because he can't beat no real man." Remo said getting up to shoot darts again.

"Remo is right though, go get your girl fuck all that waiting shit. I get what you are saying but you gone lose her to a clown. You remind me of myself when I snatched my wife up. These niggas thought I was crazy as hell how I went about it but we 3 kids in multiple businesses including this lounge and we are good. I wouldn't change shit that occurred." Nassir said patting my shoulder before taking his shot back.

"Nah this nigga ain't shit like your ass bro. Avino don't be like this nigga, I mean get your girl but his ass took the woman who drugged and robbed his ass and made her his wife after she lost her memory he went above and beyond the extreme to get her." Aasim replied cracking jokes on Nassir.

"Ahh nigga fuck you. You mad because Jade old prude ass not breaking it off to you no more, she too busies with working again. Nigga I chose the perfect wife regardless of how we ended up together it was fate and I'm about to head on home and knock her ass up again." Nassir slapped us all up before heading out. I noticed Aasim never laughed and just looked pissed at that jab his brother took at his personal life with his wife. I slapped them up and made way out as well. I had to go let Bilal know we was about to get Blue up out of here asap.

The club was lit, and our section was going off. I convinced my girls to have a night out away from our men. Blue wasn't too happy at first but then business called, and he let the shit go. I was really falling hard for him but in my gut, I was missing Avino bad. He was around but our communication was still non-existent, and it was best because Blue and I had become serious and I was practically living in his house. I sipped on my Mojito as Skai and Gianni battled it out in a twerk competition in our VIP section. My girls weren't playing with this little twerk out they were doing. I sat my glass down and joined in the fun.

A crowd around our section had formed and by the time the hit Booty went off we were worn out and laughing hysterically. We sat back down on the couches and sipped away on our drinks while some slower tempo songs started to play throughout the club. I felt vibrating near me and reached over snatching up my clutch off the sofa. I pulled my cell out and I had multiple missed calls and text messages from Blue. I blew out in frustration because he was becoming really clingy and always wanting me in the house specifically his house. I hadn't seen my god baby in a few days and tonight I planned to go home with the girls and crash and see Ricaria in the morning.

I read the messages and became even more frustrated at how many times he accused me of ignoring him. I was having a good time and he was trying to ruin the mood. I didn't respond to his messages and I put the phone on do not disturb since he had already assumed that I was ignoring him anyways. The ladies were ready to get home, so we called up an uber and gathered our things. We were stopped multiple times on our way to the door and the last time I was pulled from behind and held tightly. I knew the cologne and the feel of his hands instantly. I had missed Avino immensely, but I was too stubborn to let him know that. He rejected me and I had to move forward with life.

"Dam Brie baby I missed you. You look good as hell. I got a meeting on the top floor but just know I'm coming for you ma. Get home safe and I'm a hit you tomorrow." Avino whispered in my ear and all I could do was gasp and close my eyes at the sound of his voice. I nodded my head because I knew exactly what he was talking about.

When I opened my eyes Skai and Gianni were staring at me with googly eyes and big ass smiles. I shook my head at them and walked out the club. I saw the Uber right out front, but I also saw Blue posted up against his car across the street. I looked back to the ladies and told them to go on in the Uber and I'd be home later. I made my way to him and I could see that he was livid with me. I tried to hug and kiss him, but he turned his head and let my arms rest around his neck but never hugged me back. I stepped back observing his demeanor and debating on calling another Uber if he was gone be in a piss poor mood.

"GET IN THE CAR!" Blue yelled stepping around me and hopping in the driver seat. My gut told me to just leave and let this nigga cool off, but I ignored it and stomped over to the passenger side and hopped in. I crossed my arms over my chest after buckling my seat belt. He pulled off from the curb into traffic.

"You must take me for a joke?" His voice boomed in my ear over the music. I didn't speak because I didn't want to argue to be honest, I didn't want to talk at all.

"Blue take me home and we can talk when you calm down." I stated looking straight ahead at the road.

"Nah we are going home to my house. Fuck that shit you

talking about we gone handle this shit tonight." He replied still driving. I just sat quietly shaking my head.

We rode the rest of the ride in silence as his phone kept going off. We pulled up to his house and I hopped right out ready for a shower. I kicked my heels off and made my way up the stairs. I undid my zipper on the side of my dress and before I could pull it off Blue had me hemmed up against the door. My face came crashing into the bathroom door and I hit my forehead against the door. I felt the knot forming on my head as blood trickled down my cheek. I screamed in fear as he squeezed the back of neck tightly.

"You come up in here smelling like another nigga and then got the nerve to ignore me up in my car and house and not even try to explain your fucking self. Do you know who the fuck I am Brie? HUH?" Blue yelled into my ear loudly. I was sure my ear drum was busted from that alone. My head was banging like someone was using it as a drum and I was beginning to feel dizzy.

"I don't take disrespect lightly. You need to act accordingly when you are fucking with me and don't forget that shit. Get yourself cleaned up and wash that fucking cologne off an come show me how sorry you are for pissing me off." Blue shoved me into the bathroom and walked off. I dropped to the floor and cried my eyes out.

I don't know what I got myself into and why I was still here and not walking out that door. I questioned the way I handled things and maybe I was wrong. I was dealing with a grown man who needed a woman by his side, so I had to get my act together. I got up and got in the shower and washed my body thoroughly. I scrubbed the makeup from my face and winced at the small gash on my forehead as the water ran over it. I stepped out and turned away from my face in the mirror, but I had already gotten a glimpse of the huge knot on the left side of my head above my eyebrow and the gash across it. I grabbed the peroxide from the medicine cabinet and poured some on a cotton ball and gently dabbed my wound.

I sucked up the tears and made my way to the room where

Blue awaited me. He was laid back in the bed with his hands behind his head in the middle of the bed naked as the day he was born. I knew what he what was expected as I crawled from the end of the bed up the middle of his legs. I was not feeling up to sexing him, but I didn't want to make him more disappointed in me than he already was. I took him into my mouth slowly because my lip was still busted and swollen. I couldn't do too much but slow bob because my jaw was throbbing, and my lips were sore. Before I could even get a rhythm going, he snatched a hand full of my hair and forced my head down his pole. I gagged and gasped to breathe but he never stopped handling me roughly as he moved my head forcefully up and down.

Tears stung my eyes as he finally released his vice grip on my hair and pushed past me. He tossed me over onto my back and pulled me to the end of the bed spreading my legs roughly before entering me just as rough. I held my scream as he entered me with force. This was not pleasure and I was as dry as a desert as he kept hammering into me. He pulled out and released on my stomach and walked off to the bathroom. I ran quickly from the room as best as I could as pain tore through my lady part like someone lit a match. I went right to the guest bathroom and turned the shower on as hot as I could and stepped in. I had falling in love with a monster and I had to get away from him.

I heard my phone buzzing and I quickly stepped out the shower wrapping in a towel. I stepped into the hall and I could hear Blue snoring in the room. I quickly grabbed my clutch bag off the floor where I dropped it earlier and quickly pulled my phone out. I had a call from an unknown number, so I quickly declined it and silenced my phone. The phone lit up again and the same number flashed across the screen. I answered stepping back into the bathroom and closing the door. It was a collect call from Avino. I quickly accepted the call and waited to be connected to him.

"Brie baby you there?" His deep baritone rang out in an echo in my ear.

"Vino what's going on why are you in jail?" my heart raced as I waited on him to respond.

"Baby girl someone set us up, Bilal is in here too. We need you to go to Jorah's and have him come with you to bail us out. I'll tell you more when we out. Can you hold us down and do that?" Vino spoke into the phone sounding defeated.

"Yes Vino of course I got y'all. I'm getting dressed now." I replied slipping into the guest room and grabbing a tee and sweats out of the drawer.

I did not think twice as I hurried to get dressed. I snatched up my clutch and phone and raced downstairs. Entering the kitchen I scan the key rack and snatch up a pair of car keys. Not knowing what keys, I grabbed I hit the unlock and waited for the lights on the mystery vehicle to come on. The Range Rover lit up and took off to it hooping in. I fixed the seat and mirror and hit the garage opener button. The garage door slowly lifted, and I sped off out the driveway and to Jorah's place. I dialed up Gigi and got no answer. I called Skai and she was half sleep. I ran down everything to her and told her to get Jorah up so we could go.

Pulling in front of Jorah's and double parking I raced to the door and before I could ring the bell the trio was coming out. I was a frantic mess and tried to calm myself as I walked back to the car. Ricaria was fast asleep in Jorah's arms as he placed her in the backseat with her booster seat. Jorah kissed Skai and told her to meet him at the jail. Skai hopped in and ran down what was going on to me. Apparently, someone tipped off the feds on Bilal's trap house. They did not have any drugs, guns or money that warranted an arrest, but the illegal gambling tables were discovered in the middle of a huge game of craps and poker. Someone set the crew up, but I could not understand who or why. Despite the business they were into they gave back to the community and did a lot for the at-risk youth.

Walking out the precinct and seeing the crew made a nigga feel good. Not a lot of people where I come from had family that really had their back and best interest at heart. We weren't family by blood but that didn't mean anything these were the people I'd die for and to me that was family no matter what. I jogged down the steps and right to Brie. I picked her up hugging her tightly and inhaling her scent. I don't know who was against us but I knew I had to wrap this shit up so I could this woman right here in my arms. I went to let her down but held me tighter around my neck and I felt her tears hit my neck.

Everyone else got in the cars as we stood for a few more minutes hugged up. She finally pulled back looking deep into my eyes and then she kissed me. I noticed the sadness in her eyes when we finally broke apart. I placed her down and leaned against Jorah car as she messed around with the strings on her hoodie. I was trying to read her, but something was off with Brie. The fire that lived in her seemed to be dimmed and burning out and I hated that. I'd been following her insta she looked happy with that clown Blue for the moment. I let her live and experience dating but I was locking her down and showing how a real man handled his.

"Yo that nigga you flaunt around in my city is on borrowed time Brie Baby." I watched her blush and roll her eyes before she walked off to that nigga whip. I wasn't letting her off the hook. I followed her right to the car and hopped in. We needed to talk anyways so she could run me to the spot and then home. I put the Pandora station on Trey Songz her favorite and we rode out in silence for the first few minutes.

"Why you wait until the next nigga wife me to speak on how you feel about me and what you plan to do with me Vino?" Brie spoke taking her eyes off the rode briefly to look over at me. I turned the music down before speaking so she could hear how serious a nigga was about her little ass.

"That nigga ain't wife you if it ain't a ring on your pretty little finger. I'm setting shit up because when I come collect what's mine, I'm changing your last name and shooting your club up immediately. No games to play when I know what you worth." I spoke to her firmly as I looked her in her eyes. We were stopped at a greenlight when someone blew the horn and she finally let the breath she was holding out breaking our stare down and pulling off.

It was well into three in the afternoon when I finally let Brie drop me off and be on her way. She was acting mad weird and jumpy every time that nigga called, she ignored it but looked nervous as hell. I let her know I was serious about what I said, and I was coming to collect her real soon. I told her to tie that shit with Blue up and quick because I wasn't taking no for an answer. We knew what we both wanted, and it was no reason to be sitting back years later wondering what if.

I walked into my house and the smell of food hit me instantly. Shit I forgot I had Pilar here waiting on me last night. I wasn't in the mood to entertain her ass, but I could definitely bust down whatever she cooked and a nut as well. Pilar rounded the corner in a fire red lace bra and thong set. Pilar was Sexy as fuck but not wife material. She was cool to chill with and fuck but anything more was a no go. She better enjoys this last round because tonight she would be going home in an uber and not hearing from me again.

I was a nervous wreck as I pulled into Blue's garage. I knew he was probably pissed but this was an emergency. I took a few deep breaths before climbing out the car and making my way into the house. It was pitch black and silent inside when I stepped in. I slipped my sneakers off and quietly made my way into the kitchen from the mud room. I stopped when I thought I heard moaning, but I figured my ass was just tired. I made my way upstairs and the noises were louder. I opened the master bedroom and almost lost my balance.

My eyes burned as I watch some big tittie broad ride Blue reverse cowgirl. I saw red as I charged at the bed knocking her off him and raining blows all over him. I became infuriated as he laughed in a deep devilish tone. He pinned my arms down above my head and stared down at me. I'd socked him pretty good because his lip was a bit busted on the left side lower lip, he shook his head and pushed me down into the bed before getting up and helping the bitch up off the floor. The audacity of this nigga was making my blood boil. Granted this wasn't my house but he was my man and it was disrespectful as fuck.

I jumped up and started packing the little bit of shit I had at his house and made my way to the hallway. I felt him coming behind but I kept going because I refused to tolerate his hands he was having trouble keeping to himself and cheating, This was a deal breaker for me and I needed to get away from this situation before it became any worse. I was halfway down the stairs when Blue snatched me up by the back of my neck and slammed me into the wall, my head bounced off the wall and I winced in pain at the blow. I stared into his dark cold eyes and the look gave me chills down my spine. I had gotten myself wrapped up in the wrong type of man.

I tried to pry his hands off my neck and he only squeezed harder as I fought at him. He delivered a hit to my face so strong I temporarily blacked out. When I came back to, he had dragged me to the room and was ripping my clothes off. While yelling at the girl to get over on the bed. My eye was starting to swell shut but I was able to see the look of fear on her face.

"You want to take my shit and joy ride with your side nigga? Huh that's what the fuck you out here doing? You don't who the fuck you are dealing with huh Brie Brie?" Blue yelled as he entered me roughly.

"Nooo, I'd never do that Blue it was an emergency with my brother and my family." I cried out.

"I DON'T GIVE A FUCK IF IT WAS YO DADDY OR YOUR GRAY-HAIRED ASS GRANDMA. YOU GONE LEARN NOT TO HAVE NIGGAS IN MY SHIT." He roared as he pumped into me roughly.

I tried to hold off my whimpers, but it was no use I was pure hell as he tore into my dry center. He got off me and started tonguing the girl down as she tried to squirm away, he slapped her hard sending her to the bed next to me. I jumped back and attempted to get up, but Blue knocked me back down with his foot to the bed. I gripped my stomach in pain from the kick and cried into the bed. He had his way with her as I lay crying in the fetal position. He shoved X pills down her throat and then mine. I laid still in the bed as the pills began to take over my body. I was sore but the more the drugs settled into my system the pain was replaced with heightened hormones.

I was hot and started strip out my clothes to cool myself down. While I still had half the sense, I did things I learned to lessen the effects of the pills. I sipped from the water I had the night before on the nightstand. I tried to stay focus and not succumb to the drugs, but they were beating my ass. I felt soft hands on me and soft lips on my back. Blue yanked me back into the bed before he stood up and positioned the woman on all fours. He soft hands were still roaming my body and the touch had me on fire. I'd never experimented with women before or desired too but the way she touched my body got me intrigued.

I was high out mind and felt myself floating as her kisses trailed my stomach and her soft hands massaged my breasts. My nipples were as hard as rocks as she twirled them between her fingers. Blue entered her from the back snatching her hair into a fist and forcing her face in between my legs. She kissed and licked my thighs before spreading my lips with her tongue. When she trapped my clit between her puckered lips my head shot up and I locked eyes with Blue as she went to work. My body had betrayed me and let the drugs win. My hips rotated as she tasted every part of my womanhood.

"Make it up to daddy what you did earlier Brie. Come for daddy let Charity catch your nut Brie. You going to come for me?" Blue asked staring me down with those cold eyes.

Anger still resided in me for the way he handled me, but my body was too hot to resist the tongue lashing she gave me. And as if on command to what he asked my body took over and released a toe-curling orgasm sending my voice up a few octaves as I came. Blue smiled with lust as he watched me and not too long after he was nutting on her face. He pulled her up from the shoved some money in her hand and her belongings before sending her outside for his car service to drop her off. I hurried to the bathroom to shower and try to gather my bearings after that ordeal.

My mind was all over the place as I chastised myself for not flying out the house fast as hell before he caught me. I had to escape from this monster of a man before he killed me. The look he gave me earlier let me know he would kill me without a second thought and that terrified me. I felt the cool air as he stepped inside the shower with me. He kissed my neck and my body tensed up. He pulled me into his chest as he ran his hands down my body.

"You know I never want to harm you Brie, but you have to follow the rules if we going to work. I have business out in Las Vegas in two weeks get that eye and the bruises on your neck together and take a few days to get your mind right and you may leave Vegas Mrs. Malice." Blue Picked me up and placed my back to wall as the shower rained over us. He entered me slowly this time and took his time stroking me like he loved me. He gave me mixed signals and my twisted mind was questioning if I'd done him wrong and needed to get my act right so he wouldn't have to hurt me or teach me lessons.

I was trying to focus on working out but Nosaj took it upon himself to lay under me as I did my squats and the way he was thrusting that rock hard 10 inch pipe into my ass as I squatted was causing me to lose focus. I had five more squats to go and then onto my lunges. I was mid squat when he swooped me up and carried me to the door. He locked the door of the gym and turned the open sign to closed. I laughed as he ran to the back where his office was. Nosaj owned a few gyms and boxing clubs around New York and new Jersey. I placed me on his glass desk and kicked the door closed with his foot.

He was on me in a matter of minutes pulling my biker shorts down and off. I kicked my Air Max Trailwinds off helping him to get the shorts completely off. Nosaj had strong muscular arms and they flexed as he pulled me to the edge of the desk. I watched as he stroked his sex never taking his eyes off me. He knew the way to get me off in a matter of minutes. He slid the head up and down my wet slit before pushing the hood that hid my clit from view. He circled my clit with the tip of his sex causing me to moan out as my waters flowed freely from my tunnel.

My head felt like a bobble head as he thrust in and out of me. I gripped his arms to hold on for the ride he was about to take me on. No sooner than we got into the rhythm and I had already come numerous times someone banged on the front door and my phone rang at the same time. Nosaj didn't give one fuck except the one he was involved in currently and that was fucking the shit out of me. I tried to reach for my phone because it kept ringing and starting over but Nosaj snatched my arms and pinned them above my head on the desk.

I was heading to Brie house because no one had heard from her in a week and her phone was going to voicemail. I didn't have Blue's address or phone number, so we were really lost out here trying to locate her. Bilal was the one who was banging on the gym door and I felt like shit we had him out there for dam near an hour as we fucked all over the office. Skai had called Bilal when she came home, and Brie still hadn't returned. They hadn't seen or talked to her since the guys got bonded out of jail last week. This wasn't like Brie at all and my gut told me some foul was up and Blue was the one we needed to locate.

I knew he owned the club we were at when Brie met him, so I let Bilal know and he told Avino. Vino was losing his shit because he swore that nigga did something to Brie. He said Brie had been acting weird lately and almost as if she was scared of that nigga Blue. Apparently Blue was blowing her phone up and it had her jumpy the whole time her and Avino rode the city after he got bonded out. He let her go after about 2 hours, so I guess shit was probably bad between them but dam it's not like her to not text at the least.

I had been tearing the city up for three days now looking for Brie. This bitch ass nigga Blue was like a dam ghost around this mother fucker because no one knew where he laid his head. I had watched the club relentlessly and tonight was my lucky night. It was now almost two weeks that we hadn't seen or heard from Brie and I wouldn't get not one ounce of sleep until I found her. I felt that shit in my soul that something was wrong. Blue was leaving the club with an entourage and a gang of females. They all loaded up into the awaiting trucks and pulled off into traffic. I waited a few minutes before tailing them to their next location.

They came to a residence not too far from the club in New Rochelle. I stayed far enough back to no be noticed and I called in some reinforcement to help me handle this light work. I was about to run this nigga and his weak ass entourage for everything they had and scoop up Brie. I knew he had her tucked off and my gut told me she was in over her head. He had to cough up some answers because she was with him last. I watched as they all filed inside the home ready for the after party. I watched Blue and a female take a line right out front before stepping inside. Go figure this nigga got a powder problem. I hit Bilal. JD and Nosaj to meet me and to bring the crew.

I snatched my ski mask out the glove compartment and grabbed my Glock. As soon as I had my ski mask on the crew was pulling up behind me. I noticed a fly ass matte black Maserati pull up as well and I wondered who the hell it was. I walked up on everyone dapping up the OG Nassir, Aasim and Remo. I heard legendary tales about the way they took over Brooklyn and then New York soon after. Remo was currently the head nigga in charge after Aasim and Nassir retired and settled down with the ladies. I was shocked they was out for this move and not laid up having family movie night or some shit.

"What's good OG's?" I stated lifting my Ski mask and revealing my face.

"What's the move Vino because I can't call it?" Nassir stated slapping me five.

I ran down the details and let them know the play. I also gained insight as to why they had decided to pull up. Apparently Blue had been demoted from distributor and owed money to Nassir and had yet to pay up. Although Nassir no longer ran the streets, he still had his dealings and handled it behind the scenes. We scoped the place out from all four corners and made our move. I popped the lock off with one shot to the lock with the silencer on. All masked up and guns raised we made our way into the home. The crew handled the straggler's and club hoes while I searched for Blue.

I came to the top stairs where I heard some commotion. I eased up to a cracked door of what I assumed was the master bedroom. I couldn't see anyone, but I could hear voices arguing. I pushed into the room and Blue and some older cat were on a balcony. I pressed my body to the wall so I wouldn't be seen and made my way closer. Blue was working with the feds to take out Remo and the whole operation. I shot a text to Bilal so he could pass the info. I ducked off into the closet as the officer left out Blue got on the phone barking orders. With his back to me and distracted by the phone I stepped out and hit him in the back of the head with the butt of my gun sending him out cold.

Nosaj helped me tie him up and load him into the back of the van that Nassir had waiting. I needed to know where Brie was, and I needed answers asap. I snagged his phone and wallet and after getting an address off his ID I made my way there first to see if Brie was there. On the way I got a call from Bilal that some shit popped off and to circle to the warehouse immediately. I needed to find Brie, but I knew this shit was deep from how Bilal sounded. I exited the highway and turned around in the opposite direction to get to the warehouse.

I was awakened from my sleep by Jorah telling me to get baby girl together because he was taking us somewhere safe. My stomach was in knots because we still had not found Brie and now, we needed safety and protection. Something was not sitting right within my spirit and I hated that feeling. I'd never gone this long without at least speaking to Brie on the phone and I prayed she was safe. I gather a duffle bag full of stuff for me and Ricaria for a few days as Jorah said to. Jorah grabbed the bags I had packed and placed them in the car while I bundled up baby girl with her baby doll.

Once in the car securely we were off and into traffic. Jorah was steady barking orders over the phone and making numerous phone calls. He ended his call once we pulled into a huge estate in the wealthy part of Brooklyn. I looked at him confused and he just shrugged his shoulders and hopped out to get baby girl out the back seat. I climbed out following close behind him up the horse-shoe driveway. The house was massive and looked like something out of the luxury homes magazine I would often browse fantasizing what my dream home and life would be like.

He rang the bell and then grabbed my shaky hands as we waited. The door opened slowly, and my mouth fell open, my boss and Brooklyn's own Princess was at the door. I had taken the job at the studio as dance instructor after dancing with Aria for a while. She was a true boss ass woman with a past she overcame and that made her my Hero. She smiled at me and winked stepping aside to let us in. The home was just as gorgeous on the inside as it was on the outside. We followed her to a room that had all types of toys and a pull-out sofa was opened and set with pretty pink covers. Jorah laid Ricaria down and we all exited to the room next door. It was breathtaking with white and silver décor.

Jorah placed my bags down and pulled me in for a kiss. I grabbed him tight afraid to let go. I had no clue what was going on, but I knew it was serious and my heart was racing as my mind ran with thoughts of trouble. He hugged me back and then kissed my forehead before pulling back. He promised to check on us shortly and told me Gigi was on her way as well. He promised to find Brie and bring her home. My eyes flooded with tears and I let him go as I cried uncontrollably. Aria handed me some tissues and we talked for hours until sunup. Still no call or text from anyone I finally decided to get some rest. I couldn't sleep alone in that huge room, so I cuddled up with my baby and let sleep takeover.

I awoke to an empty bed, but the laughter of children rang throughout and specifically my baby girl. I set up stretching before reaching for my phone. I had a few missed calls from a private number and then a text from Jorah. He just text to say he was ok and that he was thinking about me. This man was so different from what I was used to, and I loved it. He made it easy to love him and fall in love with him. He had a vibe that was so cool calm and sexy it was unmatched and out of this world to me. I handled my hygiene in the adjoining bathroom before joining everyone in the family room.

Gigi had arrived and was making herself comfortable with the kids. Aria had 3 kids, Two boys and a girl. She wasted no time having babies back to back and now she said she was done and working on her career. We sat around chatting it up and playing with the kids when the bell rang. In walked two bad ass chicks that looked like models and video chicks. One went right to the kids and the children with them followed. The tall brown skin female that walked in last with her shades and nose snooted up was introduced as Jade.

Jazz was the other woman and I remembered her from the dance studio she had did our hair for a few performances.

"Excuse my rude ass sister in law she real snooty and shit." Aria stated snatching the wine bottle from jade. Jade let her shades down a bit rolling her eyes before she took a seat on the large sectional.

"Yea well I wouldn't be here if my man weren't playing captain save a hoe. We would be boarding our private Jet to the Maldives in the next few hours, but a runaway has paused all plans. They are acting like this dam girl is worth millions. She probably ran off with a nigga." Jade stated referencing Brie with Hella attitude.

"Bitch you have no type of respect. This is that girls' friends and you in disrespecting her like she done did something to you. If y'all got to go all the way to the Maldives for some sex, then your problem ain't the trip being postponed Bougie bitch. You need to get your back broke in the worst way, it's the only time I can tolerate your stuck up ass is after you been dick down and left with a smile instead of this shit you in here doing. Where is the weed at?" Jazz replied storming off towards the kitchen.

I kept my mouth shut because I knew my temper and I didn't want to be tripping in my Boss's nice ass house. But Jade had it coming one day I promised that shit. I don't play about my girls they were the only family I ever had, and I be damned if anyone fucks with them or disrespects them. I excused myself to the kitchen as well and GiGi followed but not before she bumped shoulders with Jade as Jade made her way by to the area the kids were playing in. This was about to be a long ass day.

Pulling into the driveway with my lights off the house appeared to be empty and dark. I placed my gun in the small of my back and stepped out. I crept around the house checking windows and doors. I didn't want to be obvious and go in the front door, so I picked the lock of the back-sliding glass doors off a deck to the kitchen. Once inside I quietly searched the house with my gun drawn in case Blue had any people of shooters around the home guarding it. As I made my way up the stairs, I heard ragged breathing and whimpers. I pushed the first door open and it was an empty office. Making my way to the next door I heard the whimpers and breathing loud and clear on the other side.

I pushed the door open and all the air left my lungs. I couldn't believe my Brie baby was laid tied to bed rails looking like she was near death. Her face and body were so bruised and lumped up I felt my blood boiling. I was sick to my stomach as I dropped to my knees and crawled to her by the bed on the floor where her body was laying dam near lifeless. This nigga had beaten her within inches of her life and then left her here to die. I untied her arms and legs and they just fell like dead weight. Her body was cold and weak. I grabbed a throw blanket and wrapped her body up. I scooped her up and raced out to my car.

I placed her in the backseat gently laying her down. I got in the front and started the car racing out to the hospital. She whimpered for that nigga and it infuriated me. He had her head all fucked up and I felt responsible for allowing her out into the world when I knew she was my rib. Tears clouded my eyes and anger seethed through me. I hadn't cried since my mama died and if I lost Brie, I knew I would never be ok in this world. Speeding doing 90 down the road I raced running every light to get my baby to the help she needed.

I shot Bilal a 911 text to meet me at the hospital. My phone was blowing up, but I couldn't even speak this shit over the phone and especially not right now. My focus was to get her there as quick as possible. Turning into the emergency entrance lot on two wheels honking the horn to get anyone's attention for help. Brie was fighting to breathe, and I was scared out of my mind. Throwing the car in park I hopped out and ran to the entrance yelling for help. Two male nurses rushed out with a gurney and doctors and nurses helped place Brie on the Gurney. They started working on her as they wheeled her in.

I gave my keys to a valet at the ER door and raced to see where they were taking her. I was stopped and told to wait in the family waiting room. I paced back and forth for dam near an hour before Bilal and the crew came rushing inside. I explained as much as I could while fighting to hold back the tears. We all waited for hours to here from the doctors. I was just on my way to grab an energy drink from the vending machine when a doctor came walking out. He approached me since I was the one who brought Brie in and filled out her paperwork. I couldn't hear and the room was spinning as he spoke, and the ladies began to cry as I tried to focus and read his lips as he spoke. I grabbed the wall to keep myself up from falling.

Brie was ok, she had to be ok. I didn't know what was being said but the cries of the women around me had me feeling hopeless. Bilal kicked a chair over before storming off and I still couldn't regain my composure. Nurses gathered around me and I still couldn't hear anything that they said. My ears were ringing, my heart was racing, and my eyes were burning with tears. Lord please don't take Brie baby away from us.

TO BE CONTINUED.......

L. Renee's Catalog
Losing Lyric
Once Upon A Hood Love:
A Brooklyn Fairytale
I'll Be Hom For Christmas:
A Holiday Novella
Enticed By A real Hitta 1-2
A Dopeboy's Trash
A Plug's Treasure 1-2
In My Projects: A Pine
Harbor Love Story
T.R.A.P B*tches: An
Xavier Family Story
Code Blue: Tales Of
A Shattered Heart 1
Dedicated To A Real
One: Prophecy & Cairo's
Story Coming Soon

SNEAK PEEK

MZ. LADY P
PRESENTS
Dedicated
TO A REAL
ONE
Prophecy & Cairo's Story
L. RENEE

"What do you want from me?" Prophecy asked as they stared into each other's eyes.

Cairo was nestled deep within her sugar walls atop her. Fist pressed into the memory foam mattress holding him up so that he could see her beautiful face.

"I want this" He replied while giving her a long deep stroke to her tight center causing goosebumps to form all over his body. And like it was contagious they popped up on hers as well.

"But I want this the most" He stated kissing above her supple left breast signifying that he wanted her heart.

They had been in this cat and mouse circle for quite some time now and he was ready to stake claim to his prize. He felt he earned it after the bullet to the shoulder and games she made him play to win this spot he was occupying currently it was only right. Fair exchange wasn't robbery, but he was willing to risk it all like a thief in the night just to solidify the prized possession that Prophecy was.

The admiration that Cairo held for her amazed Prophecy every time she witnessed it. She had loved a few but they never loved her like this. Cairo was the opposite across the board of what she was accustomed to. He loved her without limits and displayed it without force. She ran and dodged him to escape the unconditional love he was giving her, but it didn't work. The more she pulled the harder he went. Her heart beats freely with him and that terrified her. Then there was the age gap between them. Almost ten years his senior. A decade between them made her cringe every time she thought about it.

The thought of being a considered a cougar bothered her immensely. Cairo however never even mentioned her age. He loved her flaws and all and even after knowing who she truly was he was still ten toes down for her loyalty never wavering. That dedication couldn't go unnoticed. She flipped him with all her might onto his back mounting him with ease.

Like magnets his hands gripped a breast in each palm sensually massaging them igniting her body. Prophecy rode him like the professional jockey she truly was. Years of horseback riding she always felt was a waste came in handy when she rode Cairo. She was in pure bliss as they made love in the wee hours of the morning. Like the sound of beautiful music being created their moans filled the air.

Security held the door open as Prophecy stepped into the restaurant. As if on que the chatter ceased to whisper as the onlookers stared in awe. Prophecy had been captivating the attention of a whole room since she was a little girl. She knew the power she possessed, and the confidence exuded effortlessly. A strut as fierce as any runway model on the stage of New York Fashion Week she floated through the dimly lit restaurant walking right past the hostess.

Cairo had an important meeting that he had not let Prophecy in on. That created a feeling so foreign to her she knew all bets were off with him. Prophecy was jealous that he had a meeting with another woman. business or not she should have been present as he had been at hers many times since he forced his way into her life exclusively. After they escaped the shootout unscathed, she poured her life story and who she truly was out to him and he has been her rock since then. He refused to leave her side and if he just so happened to have no other choice than to leave her side even for brief moment, he made sure her security had back up which was his own team of shooters.

Her security had security all to ensure his precious cargo remained untouched as she ran the city literally and figuratively speaking. She laughed at his antics, but it warmed her heart. Someone so dedicated to her and not wanting anything monetary in return blew her mind. He was a man making moves of his own and operating in his own lane but still holding her down and having her back first foremost.

Prophecy strutted right over to where Cairo sat with the Brown Skin Beauty Modesty and her enormous entourage. Removing the Christian Dior CD initial shades that covered her eyes Prophecy smiled coyly before taking a seat right beside Cairo. After all that is where she belonged. Beside her man leading and running shit calling all the shots. For the past 3 months they moved as one band one sound never missing a beat or breaking a cadence. He was the drummer of her heart and it beats to tune of his. How he managed to create such a deep connection was still a mystery to her. His smooth sexy ass had swept her off her high heels and surprisingly he had not dropped her on her head like the others. This was different, the vibe felt different in her soul. This was right this blossoming relationship and he was right for her even though he eluded her today for this meeting it did not change the feelings she held but he'd get checked later on for the principal of it. She would not be Prophecy Phor Montana if she did not.

Laying eyes on Modesty after all these years was surreal. Being excluded from this intimate meeting now felt personal and purposely done. Prophecy would not call Modesty an enemy because they once were best friends as kids running the streets together. But life happened tragedy struck, and their friendship altered forever putting them against each other. A friend turned foe.

Prophecy watched as Modesty spoke about her plans and why Cairo and his Mortuary were needed. Cairo gripped Prophecy's thigh stopping her leg mid bounce. She was hot and flustered and he picked up on it instantly. She was nervous anxious and pissed off. Cairo had sensed something was off and he knew he needed to calm the beast.

Cairo's hand eased up Prophecy's leg making its way to her honeypot. Cairo smirked as Prophecy fought to keep a straight face. He introduced the two and they both nodded in acknowledgement of each other. Modesty's bodyguard whispered in her ear and Modesty excused herself from the table.

That was Cairo's que to tame Prophecy before she let loose on him. He knew she was possibly upset about the meeting he had and didn't bring her along to but two dominate ass women with huge ass egos was a recipe for disaster. Cairo Leaned in for a kiss but Prophecy mushed his face with the palm of her hand catching his lips.

So, you excluded me tonight because I have history with Modesty? Are you fucking her? Prophecy questioned while staring Cairo down through tight eyes.

"What, ha-ha girl yo ass tripping. You must be about to get yo monthly or you need some act right. I had no clue you two had a past, but I guess your personalities are similar which is the only reason I left you out was to avoid any jealous ass behavior. I am your man and you the only one I'm fucking. And watch your mouth when you talk to me it is not Lady like. Now I'm a order you a Filet mignon and Maine lobster tail dinner a glass of champagne and A raspberry tart for dessert. You sit pretty enjoy your meal let your man handle business and then I'm a take you home and bust your fine ass down. Now give me a kiss.

Cairo kissed Prophecy while massaging the wet spot of her lace panties. He was ready to call it a night so he could get lost in the warmth of her satin walls. Modesty rejoined the table and business talks resumed.

Coming soon

ABOUT THE AUTHOR

Amazon: L. Renee

Follow on Social Media
Facebook: L. Renee the author
Instagram: Lrenee418
Twitter: Poetic_Misses
TikTok: Bookmarkedwithl
Goodreads: L. Renee

BOOKS BY THIS AUTHOR

Losing Lyric

Once Upon A Hood Love: A Brooklyn Fairytale

I'll Be Home For Christmas: A Holiday Novella

Enticed By A Real Hitta 1

Entice By A Real Hitta 2

A Dopeboys Trash A Plugs Treasure 1

A Dopeboys Trash A Plugs Treasure 2

In My Projects: A Pine Harbor Love Story

T.r.a.p B*Tches: An Xavier Family Story